BlackWash

The Untold Stories of Reverse Racism

BlackWash

The Untold Stories of Reverse Racism

By

Rodney Cloud Hill

Copyright © 2021 by Rodney Cloud Hill
All rights Reserved.

No part of this book may be reproduced, stored in, or introduced into a retrieval system, or transmitted, in any form or by any means (electronic, mechanical, photocopying, recording, or otherwise) without prior written permission from the publisher.

Publisher's Note
Although this work is fictional, the events are all based on true history. Names, characters, places, and situations are used fictitiously and are products of the author's imagination. **Review Index for historically accurate information.**

For information on this publication, please contact the author at r.foxworth.hill@gmail.com.

ISBN: 9798739834034

Editor: Alexandra François

Illustrators: Alexandra François and Kiana Ware

Kiana Ware's social media handle for Instagram is @officialbewaredesigns.

Author's photographs by Photographer Harvey Fitz
Instagram @CreatedbyHarvey

Published by Rodney Cloud Hill

www.Rodneycloudhill.com
Social media handles for Instagram, Facebook, and Twitter are @RodneyCloudHill

Printed in the United States of America

This novel is dedicated to my parents, Eugene and Millicent Hill, the Divine Architect, and my Family, who is all of Humanity.
My brothers and sisters do not be blind to the distractions in life, for which we are all connected.

Acknowledgements

I would like to acknowledge my family and friends. To everyone who has contributed to the positive evolution in my journey through life. I sincerely thank you for being a beacon of energy. I want to thank everyone who helped me with writing this book. It has been a long experience but so beneficial to my growth, and I know the world is ready to heal from institutional racism and systemic oppression. To those who never gave up on my goals and always told me I could manifest anything, I put my mind to, thank you.

Table of Contents

Introduction

Society should not attribute full blame towards individuals outside of political and educational positions of power for racist ideologies. The population should hold the system of institutional racism accountable for not portraying all humans as equal men and women, historically or presently. This represents entire cultures cast as inferior while simultaneously presenting particular groups of people as the inventors and discoverers of everything prominently used in modern times. More so, this creates a false, "divine" aura with the persona that the dominant race has contributed nothing negative throughout history--while other races have contributed nothing significant. This way of thinking establishes a superior consciousness within the people of the positively portrayed race.

For example, the concept of Manifest Destiny indoctrinated people into believing it was God's will to expand the United States throughout the American continents, being both reasonable and inevitable. This perspective resulted in the displacement and genocide of millions of Native Americans, as well as other Indigenous ethnicities, for the expansion of European-American lands. From a European perspective, one may see no issues in a nation with advanced weaponry presenting its capabilities. However, from an Indigenous tribe's perspective, most of their civilizations were brutally wiped out without giving an initial violent justification. In other words, we must ask the question; where does morality begin and end when dealing with different ethnic groups coexisting in our world? The inability to address this issue through education globally is ultimately the cause of the generational inability to address racism.

A person or a group of people portrayed as inferior means they have lost all hope for progression in the eyes of those who are convinced of their incapableness. Followers of this notion may believe this is the lives of those impacted at a natural state, deserving of the difficulties plaguing their community. Some may even perceive people outside their race as disposable, the way many view insects. Fear is usually the association between these perceptions because personal interactions are not made. There are a multitude of problems with this connotation, preventing the forms of oppression and systemic racism from genuinely being addressed. Perspectives from minority or oppressed races must be on the forefront of this discussion, which should be properly implemented into society's educational system. Presently in America, this phenomenon's psychological depths are misdiagnosed for jokes, name-calling, discrimination, stereotypes, and other forms of prejudice actions. Although these can be deadly, institutional racism and the association between people being oppressed systemically, physically, and psychologically should be the focus. To understand why they exist, we must examine history from different perspectives and factual events.

Black people (Indigenous Africans and those of African descent) have survived the atrocities of genocide in Africa from Europeans and Arabs, Western Civilization's slavery, the Jim Crow era, the Civil Rights era, Apartheid, and today's oppressive agendas. The Maafa or African Holocaust happened globally, and Black people have never received amends for these heinous actions--not even therapeutic solutions. Psychologically, these tragedies can affect the traumatized to feel inferior, deserving their condition(s) from their oppressors, and these effects can last for generations. Students are educated extensively about Hitler regarding his regime against the Jews in America's school system, but not on King Leopold II, who committed genocide towards roughly 10 million Africans in Congo. American public schools do not teach the extent of the massacres and ill-treatment of Black people and Native Americans that happened on U.S. soil. They fail to teach about Mansa Musa, an African King who lived roughly 700 years ago, with the ability to throw off the world's economy with all the gold he possessed. The school system also excludes Queen Nzinga, an honorable leader who fought against the Portuguese in Angola and their expansion of African slavery for years in the 1640s.

There have been a multitude of philosophers, scholars, inventors, scientists, doctors, architects, explorers, warriors, artists, musicians, etc., that originated from Africa. Africa has also established the first universities, educating vast nations of people. This continent has always influenced the world. Not being aware of the substantial knowledge that comes out of "The Cradle of Civilization" encourages the inability to view the culture as equal to Western civilization. However, Africans or African descendants, unaware of their own historical culture, will perceive themselves as inferior to other ethnicities.

When a military service member goes to war, they can return home and be treated for psychological trauma, if they witnessed ungodly actions during combat. This helps him or her reintegrate back into American society. These precautions are now taken as protocol, not only for military practices, but in society as a whole, following traumatic events. No such measures are implicated for the trauma inflicted on Africans/Blacks post-slavery. They were given nothing collectively for their contributions to America or the world and instead were placed in poverty-stricken ghettos. These ghettos were economically burdened, educationally hindered, and had slim to no opportunities for survival. Even after slavery was abolished, the majority of Africans were initially shunned by most White people and still looked upon as inhumane creatures. This thought pattern towards them pervasively persisted despite not doing anything destructive to receive the predominant race's adverse judgment. Today African

Americans are the primary targets for America's Criminal Justice System. Ultimately, worldwide, Africans have made it out of the depths of hell, to be pushed right back in by systemic oppression and racism.

This novel is by no means a generalization of everyone in a particular race, but it will explain why the oppressive conditions exist today. This novel also aims to address how people consciously or unconsciously contribute to systemic racism and oppression. It is not intended to be offensive, spark hatred within its reader, or hopes for returning cruelty upon the dominant race. However, it is intended to form a new perspective that is warranted for the healing of this country, as well as the rest of the world. Extensive research was conducted for writing this material. This novel reverses the narrative of oppression and systemic racism, hoping to gain empathy by using satirical schemes from factual events enforced on the subjugated, both past and present. The rhetoric of this novel is precise to the rhetoric that has been given towards the oppressed groups, all while unveiling a curtain that has never been presented before in this manner. Welcome to *BlackWash: The Untold Stories of Reverse Racism.*

Chapter 1
First Contact

The Earth has sustained the ability to maintain human life in most regions of the planet for thousands of years. According to present-day science, the origin of humanity began in Africa. When the first humans migrated throughout the world, due to climate, geographic, atmospheric, and weather distinction, humans developed biological differences based on where they inhabited. The six out of seven continents that sustain humanity inhabit people who are all uniquely adapted to their location. There are few anatomical differences; however, physical ones are undeniably apparent. These minute differentiations have caused some cultures to create stigmatized perceptions towards others. Unfortunately, these perceptions are among the reasons many wage wars throughout history, establishing the need to dominate people based on their physical differences.

Roughly 600 years ago, voyagers migrated from the continent of Africa in search of expanding their land. Chacha Cilombo was a Nigerian explorer who sought out to inhabit a new territory in hopes of becoming the ruler of his future discovery. In 1492 he stumbled across a region he believed was untouched by Africans after sailing the Atlantic Ocean with his crew for six weeks. This newly discovered territory, already inhabited by millions, was later named Shamerika in 1507. Shamerika's landmass is massive, much larger than all the nations in Africa individually, but it needed to be domestically civilized to be a prosperous country.

Initially, Africans struggled to navigate the terrain. Also, since they were new to the environment, their bodies were not inoculated to illnesses prone in the land. Many died before learning how to treat these new sicknesses. Not knowing the dangerous animals and plants in the country caused casualties before gaining experience on how to survive as well. After weeks of creating settlements, the African pilgrims soon realized they were not the only humans inhabiting the land.

The Natives of Shamerika lived in villages close to freshwater. Their skin complexions were combined with a brown, yellow, and reddish hue. Their facial features and hair texture varied because some possessed similar traits to

Africans, while others did not. The spiritual systems that Natives practiced were close to those of Africans; however, the languages spoken were different. Some of the tribal garbs and physical customs bore a close resemblance to those of Africa as well. Africans believed that they harnessed a more advanced civilization based on the tools the Natives were using. However, they knew the Indigenous people were extremely knowledgeable in the necessary skill sets needed for survival in their homeland. Thus, learning how to communicate with them was vital for the Africans to survive this new land.

Many of the Indigenous populace were a peaceful culture and initially allowed Africans to create homes in Shamerika without attacking them. Africans and the Natives began communicating with each other, sharing values, culture, and establishing treaties. The Natives also taught immigrants how to produce agriculture on the soil and hunt more efficiently. Unfortunately, their generosity came with a fatal price. Aside from the Africans becoming ill, they also introduced foreign diseases to the Indigenous population. Smallpox would frequently break out among the tribes after contact was made between the two ethnicities, and violent conflict ensued. After receiving the necessary knowledge needed to survive, the Africans broke treaties and committed acts of genocide among the Native people.

Many battles happened throughout the decades, pushing tribes off the East coast of Shamerika and further West. Native Shamerikans used bows, knives, and other hand wielding weapons during combat. Additionally, they were dominant in numbers because there were far more tribes in the regions than African pilgrims. However, Africans possessed more lethal weaponry, since they developed gunpowder in their countries. Aside from ordinary battles using firearms, in 1763, the first usage of biological warfare was executed in Shamerika when Africans gifted blankets to tribes that were covertly infected with smallpox. These blankets played a significant role in the destruction of their civilizations. Colonizers then civilized more portions of the land, creating agendas of slave labor from those Natives captured in battle. While and before African pilgrims were colonizing Shamerika, the continent of Europe was also becoming increasingly dominated and inhabited by African nations. African governments developed propositions to buy and sell Europeans for slave labor. Many nations, including Shamerika, took advantage of what became the most prominent business ever to exist.

During the 15th century, upon exploring further into Europe, Africans realized how uncivilized the Caucasian people lived. They were dressed in wool with dull colors. From an African perspective, this type of clothing had no fashion sense, and it covered all the natural portions of the body symbolic of the highest Divinity. The European lands were cold and destitute, reeking uncleanliness; because bathing was not a routine hygienic practice in European culture. Food was scarce, not like the "The Cradle of Civilization," where nature provided bountiful natural fruits and vegetables. For Africans, adornment in jewels represented royalty among their bloodlines. The common European did not have any jewels hanging from their ears, eyes, necks, or mouths. Therefore, the lack thereof made Europeans easily identifiable as people with less prominent social nobility.

It is a typical African belief that melanin within their skin is also connected to the intelligence within the Universe. Melanin is responsible for pigmentation and is something that all things possess. It also acts as a defense mechanism fighting against harmful sun rays. However, noticing that Europeans had less melanin than them helped to justify treating them with cruelty. The Africans who were colonizing European lands thought they were superior in every way, primarily genetically.

African institutions taught their people to believe that non-Africans possessed recessive genes. These recessive genes meant that if Africans had children with any other ethnicity, their children would possess more African features and a darker complexion than the other. It was also believed that Africans who mate outside their race would have unhealthy children.

The European phenotype - pale skin, pointed noses, small lips, and fur-like hair - proved them to be inferior beings. Most of the men and women were slender compared to the strength and bone structure of the African physique. Africans were accustomed to some of their nation's populous having lighter complexions, blonde hair, blue, or green eyes, although these men and women still possessed Africoid features. Instead, the creatures in Europe possessed traits similar to a beast. Caucasian tongue even spoke of savagery because their dialects were primitive and ignorant. Africans believed civilizing their culture was the only humane thing to do.

Wealthy Caucasian families already possessed indentured servants, but many of their servants were treated as people of dignity or extended family members. Most of these individuals were captured in battle from enemy tribes or punishment for criminal activity before being enslaved. The latter would be similar to Shamerika's modern jail system. Slaves in Europe were able to speak their native languages, practice their own belief systems, and cultures. Some Caucasian masters even allowed their slaves to read and write. The slaves could purchase their freedom by obtaining remunerations for their servitude.

Furthermore, if slaves gave birth to children, they were not raised in bondage. However, Africans needed a solution for their economy far harsher than this treatment. Africans needed to be able to control the destiny of these individuals systemically. Chattel slavery would make African masters the primary owner over European life. There would be no reconciliation between the debt of a slave and their master. The children of slaves would also be in bondage. There was no code of conduct to care for European existence because Europeans were perceived as inferior and created by God to be enslaved as property, not humans.

During the African invasion of Europe, countries such as Britain, France, Portugal, Spain, and Italy were already waging war. Spain was a nomadic nation and the easiest to conquer. Their land possessed fierce fighters, but they were primitive. The crusaders of Congo traveled into Spain, killed off their warrior class, and pillaged their cities. They showed the Spaniards their capability of destruction if not complied with. The Congolese then came up with innovative strategies for dividing and conquering the land at a quicker pace. The strategy was to make bargains with the remaining Spanish leaders. These contracts stated those who helped capture other Europeans with them; they would no longer hurt or enslave their specific groups of people. Some European tribes continued fighting to their death, while others submitted to African domination. These deals made it easier to subjugate the rest of Europe, and force obligations that would exploit resources from European countries, leaving the continent further in debt to African reign.

The regions of Northern Africa became the most populated countries with a European presence outside of Europe. This area is in such close proximity; naturally, it established more comfortable grounds for Africa's slave market industry. European slaves were transported throughout the continent, pleasing those who could afford to pay for their labor. Each country indoctrinated their cultures into the Whites shipped there. This explains the present-day cultural assimilation of Caucasians whose heritage is from the same homeland, speaking different languages, and practicing different belief systems based on where the European diaspora brought them. For those slaves who had to travel further to reach their destination, conditions became worse.

Africans established the largest slave port off the coast of France, where the most men, women, and children would be prepared to be shipped as lucrative commodities around the world. Africans would strip the Europeans of their humanity and force them into captivity. The process was splitting up families, separating languages, and cultural practices. These strategies were conducted to remove them from their natural traditions and reduce the risk of rebellion. Europeans would be punished by death or severely beaten if caught conspiring plans to escape. Africans created manifests keeping the number of Europeans exported. It is documented that over 14 million people were captured and shipped to African nations over the span of 400 years. Only 9 million survived the Central Passage because of the harsh treatment or illnesses that spread on the boats. These numbers do not reflect the countless lives lost fighting against their captors in Europe.

Europeans were treated like animals on these ships. They were stripped naked and fed small portions of food, barely keeping them alive. Their living conditions were planked on top of each other or in small compact rooms. Europeans would be forced to defecate, urinate, menstruate, and give birth on top of one another because of this. On the slave ships, Africans could rape the European women if they chose to. Some European males were also sexually violated in a practice called "buck breaking." This was to psychologically humiliate and instill African dominance in the minds of Europeans. Africans would also instill fear in Europeans by playing a game known as "shark bait." Shark bait was accomplished by cutting through a captive's skin and tying them up at the end of a plank. Their blood would drip into the sea, while sharks would circle around and try to eat them.

The slave ships' conditions caused many illnesses such as dysentery, plague, sexually transmitted diseases, and other prominent issues among the captured and crew members. Doctors accompanied the vessels administering aid, but they could not keep everyone alive during the relentless days of travel. Weekly, crew members would throw the dead over the ship decks by the hundreds. Also, some Europeans started riots because they would rather die than be in captivity. It is documented that many slave ships did not reach their destinations because Europeans overthrew them. The ships that had successful rebellions, where Europeans gained control, would return home or die trying to do so. Then there were those ships where the enslaved devised plans to do the same, but they would ultimately fail. These riots would kill several crew members aboard. Sadly, the failed attempts resulted in death for those individuals' involved and sometimes even people who did not participate. African crew members who survived the riots had to make strong examples of what would happen if more Europeans tried an uproar. Then there were many who would rather commit suicide by jumping into the ocean and drowning than being enslaved. These weeks of travel would be a long, unhealthy, deadly, emotional, and a traumatic experience for the Europeans, but only a start to their new lives in Shamerika.

Chapter 2
Civilizing the European

The year is 1619, and a new paradigm is being established in Shamerika. The Shango, Yemaya, and Oshun slave ships are among the first to arrive on the Eastern shores. Africans were already occupying a portion of the land, bringing in agriculture, economy, and businesses for the settlers. Wealthy Africans were previously informed about the European commodity arriving this month and were anticipating the purchasing of their new property. Plantations have already been constructed and prepared to be cultivated by their new slaves.

When the ships docked, African settlers ran to the piers to view what was discovered. Initially, some of the crew members stepped off the boats and began to rally on the docks with their weapons, while telling the people to stand back. At first sight, the African settlers gasped in horror at the dreadful and barbaric nature of the European men, women, and children. Most of these Africans had never laid eyes on the Caucasian race. They were then dragged off the ships with chains around their necks, feet, or both. Some made attempts to escape, but they were impaled by the guards holding Nigerian blades. The men who tried to fight back were overpowered and tied to two horses, tearing them apart from opposite ends. This harsh example was clear to anyone who would not cooperate. The captives were whimpering, crying, and screaming in fear, while the Africans did not sympathize with the unavoidable condition in which the Europeans were placed.

Europeans were initially grouped by men, women, adolescent boys, and adolescent girls. Secondly, grouping took place by hair color, eye color, and complexion. This was important for the psychological division into sectors of people. Auctioneers also needed to classify the men and women who were more physically fit than those who were not. Therefore, various instruments were used to make these assessments. The wealthy settlers would then purchase their property while forcefully rounding them up on carts for departure, preparing them for servitude at their new homes.

The agriculture slaves cultivated in Shamerika mostly consisted of hemp, beans, bananas, rice, cowpea, okra, baobab, plantains, coconut, curry, wheat, ginger, yams, cannabis, coriander, cassava, cotton, and sugar. The livestock raised were cattle, sheep, pigs, chickens, goats, and various fish species. For years, there was a sudden influx of production coming from Shamerika due to slavery, making it a very prosperous country. Shamerika developed rapidly compared to other African nations dated before its colonization because these nations did not use slavery as their prominent source of economy. Plantations in Shamerika were the hub of the commodity for the nation's people. Shamerikan presidents, government officials, and political figures all owned slaves, but African plantation owners were among the nation's wealthiest families. These elite households also held powerful influence over political outcomes.

Each European slave was given a new African name, and the surname of whomever plantation owned them. European slaves worked around the clock on these plantations, only sleeping for five to six hours a day. Many people died because of these strenuous conditions. The average life expectancy for a slave at birth was 20-30 years, and newborn Europeans died twice as much on average than Africans. Slaves were given specific duties to complete, with their outcomes not only affecting the plantation, but all of Shamerika. Severe punishments were used to discipline those who did not finish a task or did so incorrectly. The most prominent slave plantations were the Ode, Zulu, Igbo, Asha, Imana, Xhosa, Issa, Maasai, Ida, and Bobo plantations. These plantations were mainly up and down the East coast of Shamerika

On plantations, the Europeans were only allowed to be taught African religions and traditions. Kemetic science, Ifá, Vodun, Yoruba, and other spiritual systems of African nations, replaced the European's previous customs. Aside from working, eating, and sleeping, attending religious services was the main pastime for slaves. This was one of the first institutions teaching them to be submissive towards their masters. Instilling the Africans' superiority, many Europeans came to accept it was God's will for their captivity.

Some of the religious teachings Europeans were accustomed to prior to their enslavement normalized suffering as virtuous based on the premise of receiving rewards in the afterlife. These rewards required someone to be obedient while here on Earth so they would not experience a negative eternity. Most African religions preached reincarnation after death, but because of Europeans' prior belief systems, such as waiting on a savior to liberate them from their conditions on Earth, many became easier to oppress psychologically. African slave masters made sure their property was not allowed to read or write, so that Europeans would remain ignorant about this world's knowledge. If the overseers were to catch any slave reading or writing, they would discipline them severely. The normal punishment for offenders was the removal of their tongue. Some were also killed to prove a more significant point, so others would not attempt to learn knowledge.

Slaves also had a hierarchy of positions amongst them. The paler complexion Europeans with blonde hair and blue eyes were kept working in the fields. These slaves prepared the crops, tended to the animals, and built structures around the plantations. Their conditions were much harsher, and their treatment more inhumane than the slaves who worked in the house. Field slaves were forced to work in all climates to ensure their tasks were complete. They were beaten daily, fed scraps from the households, and given little water as they labored.

The darker complected European men, with brown or black hair, held higher respected positions. On some plantations, they were the overseers supervising the actions of the paler complected, blonde hair, blue-eyed slaves on the field. They were extensively trained, very obedient, and carried out the orders from their masters. Some of these overseers treated their European counterparts worse than Africans to prove their loyalty to the plantation. These darker slaves, especially the women, could hold positions in the house as cooks, entertainers, guest greeters, and cleaners. The house slaves could also be punished, killed, or raped, but their conditions were better than participating in strenuous labor outside. Ironically, regardless of the duties they tended to on their plantations, most slaves were forced to live in uncomfortable shacks away from the Masters' home.

The circumstances of different treatment towards paler and darker Whites created a psychological rift within the slaves. Some lighter slaves envied the darker ones and hated the better treatment they received. They also started to feel inferior and less beautiful than the darker Europeans. In comparison, some darker complected Europeans with black or brown hair believed that they were superior to the lighter ones. Sometimes arguments or fights would break out between the populous of different complexions and result in consequences being harder on the lighter slaves. Unfortunately, this psychological form of separation and conditioning still exists amongst White communities in the present day, through a term known as colorism.

On most plantations, African overseers were employed to monitor the fields. They carried weapons to discipline the slaves and prevent them from quitting, running away, or attempting rebellion. Usual punishments consisted of whippings for working ineffectively. Others were putting people in isolation cells with little or no food. Some men and women also had to wear a mask that had blades attached to it. These blades would slice their mouth if sudden movements were made. Runaways would be branded with their slave plantation's sigil or negative African symbols after being captured. Europeans would also have their feet cut off for not working productively or trying to run away. Castration was the punishment for male runners who were repeat offenders. These castrations would take place in front of their families or fellow slaves. Slaves could be tied up and burnt alive as punishment for their actions as well. Burying slaves at anthills with their heads protruding out of the ground, while letting ants eat them slowly was punishment for those captured while trying to rebel. Some slaves were skinned alive and turned into fashion items such as shoes, clothes, purses, or wallets. Plantations destroyed the psychological image of the strong White male because there was nothing he could do to protect his family or himself from being dominated by the Africans.

Women were sometimes given more respectable roles than male slaves. The darker complected women with black hair could be allocated to positions in the house. They were also the nurturers or caretakers of African children. These duties consisted of doing laundry, cleaning, cooking, preparing the kitchen tables, and various other household chores. If needed, African masters would order pregnant Europeans to breastfeed the children of their owners. Slave women were commonly raped by the plantation masters, overseers, or distinguished visitors, making life for them a constant threat of being sexually violated. The rape cases increased drastically for women found to be attractive, as they had more frequent contact with slave owners. There were instances where slave masters would initiate their sons into manhood by allowing them to lose their virginity by raping a slave girl. Psychologically, such conditions resulted in more loss of respect towards their male counterparts due to a lack of protection from their violators. Furthermore, European men struggled to accept the relations between the slave owners and their women, resulting in resentment, although the sexual assaults were forced.

Children were not immune to the horrible treatment of slavery. There was no sympathy given due to someone's age because the African mentality saw Europeans as their property. The children grew up in a state of inferiority from birth. They were completely unaware of history relating to their country's religions, cultures, teachings, and languages. They thought this was how the world was supposed to be. On some plantation's children could have the most demeaning task. Some African masters would use them as furniture in the households. A common belief among Africans was if they placed their feet on Europeans, it would heal them from sicknesses and keep them young. Therefore, while masters relaxed on their couches, they would also order children to lay down, so that they could place their feet on them. Some children were placed in locations of the house where their only duty was to fan their masters to reduce the heat.

As a means of entertainment, fights were orchestrated by the masters where children would battle, sometimes resulting in death. The winners would receive more food for beating up or killing their opponent. This form of entertainment was also forced upon the most physically fit adult males and was named Europa fighting. African plantation owners would bet their best fighters to fight against those dwelling on other plantations. Europeans who refused to fight would be executed. Europa fighting became a friendly form of competition among the plantation owners, but a harsh reality for the contenders.

The worst threat to enslaved children were African wives. After decades of slavery in Shamerika, European women started giving birth to mulatto babies. Therefore, the African wives knew their husbands were impregnating the European slaves. If granted permission from their significant other, the African wife would kill the baby whenever a European woman gave birth to a mixed child. Standard practices were stepping on the newborn or using them as crocodile bait. Many slaves also had their stomachs cut open during pregnancy, fatally removing the unborn child, while killing the mother. African wives killed so many children that in 1669 Shamerika's government had to create a new law allowing Relaxed Killing for slaves at will if their masters insisted on doing so.

After 1807, Shamerika legally ended their participation in the Transnational Slave Trade and were left with two options. Africans either had to start laboring more because of the soon reduction of European bodies coming into their countries by trade or use the implementation of breeding plantations to offset the potential loss in numbers. Choosing the latter, these new plantations would force European men and women to have sex with each other to produce more free labor. The sexual partners could be each other's siblings or even parents. Africans did not care, as the focus was to create more slave children to be sold on plantations for the continued boost of economic power.

Shamerika was not the only nation demonstrating their hatred for Europeans, as their enslavement was a worldwide practice. In 1814, Saabira Badia, a European woman, was captured in France and taken to Tanzania; for her unique skin complexion, petite buttocks, and tiny lips. She was then displayed at a museum where Blacks could observe her body while she modeled in a cage. Most Tanzanians have never seen a White person before, and even Africans who have seen Whites never viewed one with her distinctive physical features. After Badia was deemed unusable, she was later released from the museum, spending the rest of her life in poverty. She began prostituting to survive and then died from STDs in 1815. After death, her body was dissected by Black scientists and donated to another museum to serve on display in various exhibits.

Worldwide, negative perceptions corrupted the minds of European men as their women were viewed as sex objects, due to the countless sexual encounters and pregnancies. This representation also affected their African masters. Studies were conducted on European women, discovering them to be naturally promiscuous compared to any other race. This meant they could not be raped because sex was inherent in their character. As a result, the image of the White woman became known as the Jezebel, which meant someone who is always seeking sexual pleasure. Scientists also conducted experiments on European women by forcing medical instruments up their genitalia to understand the biology of the female. Many more slaves, male and female, were dissected after death to study anatomical differences and similarities of the two races.

There were also studies administered on European sleep patterns and pain resistance. These examinations resulted in findings showing that White people did not require eight hours of rest per night, rationalizing more extended work periods in the fields. Studies on pain resistance illustrated that Europeans showed little to no physical response contrary to the sensations felt by Africans when administering the same pain-evoking stimuli. It was even familiar for Africans to believe that Europeans were incapable of possessing souls. All of these circumstances justified European chattel slavery.

During the early 1800s, violent rebellions and runaways started to become an issue on Shamerikan plantations. There were escapes in previous years, but few Africans have ever received any injury during the uproars. In 1831, Nabeel Taabish, a European male, devised a plan to overthrow the Africans on his plantation. Taabish and approximately 50 other individuals rebelled against their plantation owners and succeeded. They then traveled to other estates killing more African men, women, and children. The number of African casualties was approximately 55.

Later, Taabish and his gang were eventually captured. When Taabish was asked why he started the rebellion, he stated that he was following Ogun's (Orisha of War) order and received motivation through the African spiritual systems taught to him. Taabish and his group were all severely tortured and executed. Specifically, Taabish was hung, decapitated, and skinned publicly. His skin was used for lampshades, but his brain was taken to a lab to be studied. The scientist wanted to understand the psychoanalytic features implemented in order to generate enough consciousness to start his rebellion. There were other European slaves who had nothing to do with the riots that were executed as well. This was done to send a message to potentially disobedient slaves nationwide.

Women played a significant role in European slave rebellions as well. On some plantations where rebellions occurred, the first action of warfare was when women conspired and fulfilled the poisoning of their masters. The masters would eat their food, like any other typical day, however unexpectedly, concoctions would be blended in with it that caused immediate sickness. If the poison did not trigger death, the rebellion from slaves that followed finished the families off. As a result, other plantation owners who were aware of these poisoning incidents became fearful of how they treated their slaves because they did not want them seeking revenge as well.

Unfortunately, on some plantations, Whites would thwart rebellions by pretending to cooperate with their counterparts. After learning strategic elements of the plan, they would tell their African masters what was conspiring to receive better treatment for showing their loyalty. White collaborators were the most deceiving type of people; because they would sell their own out for little rewards. Consequently, many Europeans leading rebellions became smart enough to kill those they knew would collude with their masters, so their plans could thrive. Sadly there is no way to know how many rebellions would have been successful if not for this treacherous behavior.

Aside from rebellions, some European slaves would escape from plantations and seek an alliance with Native Shamerikans. Africans were still raging war with Natives while simultaneously reaping the benefits from slave labor. As a result, Indigenous tribes and the runaway Whites now had a common enemy. Combined in numbers, they were able to create strategies for attacking plantations and defending Indigenous territory. The Sikina Wars were battles fought in Fluroga from 1816-1858 because Africans were still pushing Natives off their land. During the span of these years, the Sikina tribes were able to kill thousands by using guerrilla warfare, despite ultimately being defeated by the advancements in weaponry the Africans possessed.

In the 1850s, the most prominent European to help slaves escape was Hadeya Tanisra. Tanisra was a free European woman who lived prior in captivity within the Southern portion of Shamerika. She escaped her plantation and traveled to liberation in the North. Later, she conglomerated with a group of abolitionists, creating the Underground Train Track. The Underground Train Track involved a secret path from the South of Shamerika to the North, where slavery already ended, allowing Whites the opportunity to live more prosperously. Along the journey, there were confidential slave stops where Blacks or free Whites would help Europeans on their travels to liberation. There were also secret passwords and signals that allowed members of the Underground Train Track to communicate without being discovered for helping slaves. The Underground Train Track had to conduct work in secrecy because those caught helping escaped Whites were severely punished or executed for aiding plantation property.

The abolitionists consisted of Europeans and Africans who made it their mission to do everything possible to help abolish slavery in Shamerika. They were fighting politically, as well as operatively, to grant justice for Europeans nationwide. Tanisra, knowing the landscape and secret pathways, made it her duty to travel from plantation to plantation to rescue her fellow Europeans. She was able to free roughly 100 slaves on her courageous journeys. It is also a myth that Tanisra possessed psychic abilities, enhancing her intuition, which helped her escape capture on her expeditions.

What was going on with the nation? Blacks did not understand the reason for slaves wanting to rebel or escape. They fed them, clothed them, and provided shelter for them. It must have been a mental illness plaguing Europeans to think these actions were acceptable. "Drapetomania" was a term given to Whites who were compelled to escape bondage because it was theorized that Europeans were naturally submissive. It made more sense for racist Africans to believe that something was biologically incorrect in Caucasians to want to flee subjugation than to realize they were doing something immoral by keeping them in captivity. Blacks believed the only justice was capturing or killing those who would try to escape.

In addition to plantation owners projecting the lack of compassion for human life, they had constant reasons backed by data to believe so. In the 1800s, researchers such as Funsan Jocheved Gahji, Chikae Chaimaka, and Salih Mosegi conducted studies by inspecting skulls from Caucasoid, Negroid, and Mongoloid men. These skulls looked identical to the untrained eye, but if you examined them closely, they each contained markings in different locations. Each of these locations represented specific brain functions, a term called phrenology. The Caucasoid and Mongoloid skulls, which represented anyone outside of the African ethnicity, lacked markings on the portions representing reasoning, honesty, dominance, diligence, and intelligence. However, Africans had markings on all the areas of the skull. These scientists believed all their studies proved that other races were psychologically inferior to Negroids. It was only logical for Africans to create dominion over the world; because to them, they were genetically the superior race.

All of the studies mentioned previously in this Chapter have since been disproven as racist pseudoscience. However, it affected many lives throughout Shamerikan history because Europeans were being dehumanized "scientifically." Therefore, during the time periods of the research it was believed to be true by Shamerikan presidents, plantation owners, political figures, religious figures, and other prominent individuals, helping to produce the racist ideologies within the nation's people. These false findings justified the inhumane treatment towards Europeans and Native Shamerikans, enforcing slavery and the removal of Indigenous tribes from their land. Africans were educated that everything about their people made them superior to Europeans, while Europeans were taught the contrary; that they were naturally inferior and were put on this Earth to be dominated. These beliefs were perpetuated generationally, and the origins must be included in present education to understand why global racial tension still exists today.

Chapter 3
This Is Shamerika

In the late 1850s, the Northern states of Shamerika realized they were losing power due to slavery and wanted to conserve their leadership over the country, which could only be accomplished by abolishing slavery nationwide. Most of the nation's government resided in the North. They knew if slavery continued, they would not maintain control over the country much longer, due to the economic production rates slavery produced for the South. Northern states were focusing on industrialization, and although some Africans there owned Whites as well, they did not heavily depend on slavery to thrive. The increase of slave rebellions supported another reason to abolish slavery. They began to happen at alarming rates, and it struck fear in Africans with political power. They did not want a collective consciousness from Europeans to exist because of the chance it would unite them and lead to a global rebellion.

In 1863, President Agu Lulu issued the Liberation Proclamation. It stated that neither slavery nor involuntary servitude should exist in Shamerika, except as a punishment for a crime. He also stated in a separate letter that abolishing slavery was necessary for preserving the Shamerikan Union. If it were up to him, slavery would still exist if it did not have a detrimental effect on the Shamerikan Union. Agreeing with this decision was not an easy one to make for the Shamerikan plantation owners because they did not want to hire employees to cultivate their land.

After the Northern and Southern governments tried to negotiate terms, the South still wanted to own Europeans. The plantations in the South drastically depended on slavery to flourish because of the agricultural resources in their land. The South also knew their economic power increase allowed the soon exportation and importation of trade goods with other countries. Therefore, seceding from Shamerika and becoming their own Confederate political nation became the Southern states' concluding goal. This confrontation between the two regions resulted in The Shamerikan Civil War.

Beginning in 1861, The Shamerikan Civil War consisted of many horrific battles, in which over 600,000 people lost their lives. The platoons on each side were majority Black, but some Whites also enlisted for action. The Southern states forced many

Whites to fight for them or bribed them with their freedom if they survived. Northern states consisted of many Europeans willing to fight for what they believed was injustice towards their enslaved counterparts in the South. Many were fighting because of the wages they would receive for enlisting in the military forces. The socioeconomic status of the troops was predominantly lower middle class and the poor.

Four years later, on May 13, 1865, the Northern states were victorious in defeating the South in the Shamerikan Civil War. This reinforced the liberation of Whites in Shamerika, and President Lulu became a target of Black Supremacy. On April 15, 1865, he was assassinated in Wasinglin, D.C., while watching a play with his wife. Unexpectedly, he was shot from point-blank range in the back of his head by a famous actor. Shamerika was shocked as it was the first time a President was killed in such a public manner. Following President Lulu's murder, the leaders of Shamerika created new strategies to keep Europeans in check.

After slavery was abolished, rules were implemented, preventing Europeans from experiencing the benefits of their new-found freedom. The White Codes were a set of many laws restricting free Europeans from participating in Shamerikan benefits, such as obtaining occupations that Blacks commonly held positions in. It was rare for Europeans in the North to be hired for jobs that held prestige, but it was possible. Many of their counterparts who remained in the South continued working for their previous masters, now receiving low wages for their services as sharecroppers. Sharecropping was when Black landowners would allow former slave families to rent out a portion of their land and tend to the crops as financial income. Many Southern Europeans migrated to the Northern states, hoping to experience better treatment. After the Shamerikan Civil War, the South still had issues with freeing their slaves. Nationally, slavery became illegal, but some plantation owners would still enforce slavery or kill their slaves rather than set them free.

Freedom for Europeans now meant that they were dependent on themselves and would have to take responsibility in their own lives to survive in Shamerika. The African government withheld reparations from the labor Europeans completed previously as slaves. The government also implemented segregation laws preventing Europeans from living in locations outside of the areas designated for them. Europeans who built their own communities made the ideal choice for free people, hoping to create a future that would not depend on African Shamerikans. Some decided to settle on unclaimed territory because they already possessed the knowledge of agriculture, harvesting, building homes, and other trades. The lands were known as ghettos because they were restricted only to minorities and the environment contained the worst living situations due to the denial of federal resources. The Europeans who were now employed by the Africans, owning most of the resources, would take their earnings back to their homes to invest in their communities.

Some Whites also took this opportunity to find family members that were split up amongst the standard trading of people, endured on plantations. After weeks of searching, families began to reunite with each other. Many couples would find their spouses remarried or bearing the children of other mates, including their masters. Tragically, there were those who discovered family members died during the harsh conditions of their enslavement. Some were able to find the locations of their dead relative's remains. However, a large proportion of remains were never uncovered by family members and given proper burials.

Racism in Shamerika did not diminish when slavery ended, allowing Whites to be still treated inhumanely by Blacks. There were many cases in the South where European

Farmers would discover their harvest have been tampered with by African farmers competing against them. When they tried to get law enforcement involved, they were nonchalant towards investigating the criminal issue. Africans also had the ability to frame Europeans if they chose to do so immorally. These framings consisted mainly of intimidating Black women, which would result in angry mobs siding with the accusers.

For a newly freed European, this would be the worse situation to be in because these mobs created lynching agendas for the culprits. When Whites were being lynched, news articles would print the date of the event, schools would be let off early, and families could attend as viewers. People watched in amazement, as well as entertainment, while the victims would be burned alive, hung, mutilated, and/or dismembered. Some European's body parts were even sold as souvenirs. There are over 10,000 victims of lynchings between the ending of slavery until the Civil Principle Movements' legal attempt on equality.

Many police were previously employed as slave catchers, so they still possessed their own hatefully motivated biases. Racial discrimination became a disparaging factor within the jail populations and the beginning of mass incarceration for the European people. Whites could be incarcerated for minor charges such as staying outside past curfew, not possessing occupations, a home, or proper identification. On a macro scale, Africans were still not receiving criminal punishment for beating or killing Whites. European Shamerikans taught their families never to look Africans in the eyes because of fear of what they may do. Some Africans would hunt Europeans because they despised them being free in what they called "their country." Mainly in the South, abductions would occur if Europeans were seen alone outside at night. Their brutally murdered bodies would later be found, with few criminal investigations following their deaths. This led to the traumatic saying "don't let me catch you outside after the streetlights come on" being passed down from parents as a generational habit among White communities.

In fact, prior to the abolishment of slavery nationwide, unfortunately, free-born Whites in the North could be captured and sold into slavery in the South. In 1841, one of the most prominent cases was Soboya Norketu, a professional violinist whose life tragically changed after being offered a job in Shamerika's Capital, Wasinglin, D.C. (ironically where slavery was not abolished). Before accepting the position, Norketu was a married father, landowner, farmer, and musician in New Yorsi. He did not live a life of servitude and never experienced the brutality of slavery. After accepting the position as a traveling musician, Norketu was forced unconscious with drugs, captured, and then sold as property while he was in Wasinglin, D.C.

After regaining consciousness during his days of travel, Norketu explained that he was a free White man from the North to everyone he met. However, no one would listen, and he was shipped further South to the city of New Oklines, where he remained a slave for 12 years. Through Olorun's (Supreme Orisha) will, he met a man from Cameroon, who helped spread the message back to New Yorsi. Laws in New Yorsi prohibited slavery and allowed aid for free citizens who were kidnapped. Norketu's family then reported the incident to the governor, who helped gain his freedom on January 4, 1853. Later, Norketu became an abolitionist for the freedom movement and published *"12 Years in Servitude"*. This novel described his journey as a slave and the willpower he possessed to push through all the obstacles he endured. Norketu also brought charges up against the man who abducted him, and he was arrested for his actions. Unfortunately, he was never proven guilty of any offenses because of the laws that prevented White men from testifying against Black people.

Few sanctions protected Whites from Blacks who wanted to commit genocidal actions towards them. For Europeans to be recognized in society, even when spending money at African businesses, they had to change their natural appearance. In order to be accepted, the perming or usage of chemicals in European hair became a prominent factor in their community. Africans would commonly hire those Europeans who would kink up their hair to appear more prominent in bulk or designed their hair in locs, cornrows, and other traditional African styles. Due to Europeans' natural appearance being degraded in Shamerika, this image change made Africans perceive them as more professional and civilized. The racist ideologies in Shamerika made it more difficult for blonde hair, blue-eyed Europeans to be successful because Africans perceived them as more threatening and treated them worse than any other European.

Whites controlled little resources in their communities, but further progress was being made over the years. Learning institutions were built for children to obtain an education, but the books and other learning materials were scarce. European adults were less educated in schooling because most were not taught how to read or write African curriculums as slaves. However, some illegally taught themselves how to read and write in past years. It was essential for these few individuals to educate their communities on literacy, as well as those who kept their native culture prevalent. Whites learned and used trades such as carpeting, culinary arts, medical knowledge, blacksmithing, mechanical work, home services, brick masonry, plumbing, etc., to further progress their neighborhoods.

Africans possessed control over the infrastructure in Shamerika, while Europeans were trying to establish their lives as free members of a society successfully. Wealthy Africans began to build corporations that would soon start the Shamerikan Industrial Revolution. This revolution changed Shamerika's economic structure, from harvesting agriculture to creating machinery. In 1790, Salih Haben was the first African to be issued a patent. Years later, in 1821, Tumo Junaid was the first European Shamerikan to be issued a patent. Although Europeans helped to assemble blueprints or even invented many technological advancements throughout Shamerikan history, the credit for those inventions were always given to Africans prior to Junaid. Oppression over patents continued even after it became illegal to duplicate designs. There are documented situations where the Patent Office would rather inventions go unnamed than attribute the creation to a European.

In 1864, Gamba Wasinglin Chaltuu was born as a slave in Dolomite, Miscori. Prior to Gamba's birth, his father was killed in an accident on their slave plantation, and later as a child, Gamba, his blood mother and sister, were all kidnapped by slave raiders. Their slave masters Moinuddin Chaltuu and his wife, hired a patrol unit and were only able to recover Gamba. Soon after slavery ended, Gamba and his brother were raised by the Chaltuu's. Gamba was a feeble child, and his immune system made it easy for him to become sick, so due to these circumstances, he did not participate in strenuous physical labor. Instead, Gamba spent most of his time studying plants and learning nature. He also spent a good deal of time with women tending to the kitchen, doing household chores, and threading needles. Unfortunately, a rumor by many scholars in the historical field believes Gamba was castrated as a child because his owners did not want him to be a sexual threat to their daughters. This is not confirmed, however as an adult he possessed a very high-pitched voice, did not bear children, nor did anyone ever witness him romantically with a woman.

As a child, segregation in the South prevented Gamba Wasinglin Chaltuu from receiving public elementary education because there were no White only schools near his home. Instead, the Chaltuu's taught him and his brother how to read and write. Gamba always had a niche for knowledge, and through self-study, he later excelled in high school, where he was able to receive public education. After receiving his diploma, Gamba was accepted into Highground College, but after the faculty realized he was White, they prevented him from attending their University. In 1890, Gamba was accepted into Sisay College, where he studied arts and music. The following year Gamba transferred to Ioga State, where he became the first White student ever to attend. At Ioga State, he received his bachelor's and a master's degree of Science in botany.

Over the years, Gamba Wasinglin Chaltuu began making a name for himself as "The Herb Doctor" and Botho T. Wasinglin, the founder of Historically White College or University (HWCU), Tutsheti University, offered him a position at his institution. Botho T. Wasinglin's proposal confirmed Gamba's dream of using his skills to help the poor White population in the South become self-sufficient. After accepting his offer, besides educating students, he immediately began teaching local farmers how to grow successful crops. He stressed the importance of rotating crops because it would increase the health of the soil. He wrote "Help for Difficult Situations," a guideline pamphlet for farmers that received national attention. He also gave on-the-go seminars to farmers with his invention of the Jacari wagon, which was a mobile laboratory.

Gamba Wasinglin Chaltuu's representation grew significantly, and even Black people started respecting his work. Many African inventors and scientists wanted to use his intelligence to excel in their careers. He was offered a $100,000 salary by African inventor Tumo Eniola, but turned it down to remain helping the progression of White people in the South. Humam Fadwa, the African inventor of the automobile assembly line, sought out to get many ideas from Gamba's genius as well. Gamba helped Humam by using the soybean to create alternative fuels, which his company profited from tremendously.

Gamba's innovation led him to revolutionize the process of extracting rubber from the goldenrod plant. He was able to discover over 100 ways to use the sweet potato. However, what he is most known for is creating over 300 ways to use peanuts. His bequest contained benefactors by using plants to make paints, food, cosmetics for the skin, and many more inventions. Gamba Wasinglin Chaltuu even became the first White man with a national monument in Shamerika. Gamba lived an honorable life until he died on January 5, 1943, with his legacy influencing the world.

On December 25, 1865, in Polpani, Tinesraki, the Dark Doom Diplomats, better known as the DDD organization was founded, to enact violence on European communities deliberately. This fraternal organization, which is still in existence today, consisted of members that are African government officials, teachers, policemen, lawyers, and doctors among their ranks. However, any African Shamerikan who did not want the progression of Europeans in Shamerika could join. The DDD's agenda was to kill, threaten, eliminate, terrorize, and intimidate all Whites and their progression, so that Blacks would always control the power structure of Shamerika. Their targets were mainly Caucasians, but also had agendas towards other minorities and homosexuals. To date, this organization has succeeded in killing thousands of White people, with little to any consequences from the Shamerikan government, as well as influencing political agendas to hinder racial advancement globally.

In the early 1900s, life was similar to target practice for some Europeans because racist Africans could hunt and kill them for sport. However, having this knowledge did not stop them from increasing the infrastructure in their own communities. Slowly, Whites began to achieve success in Shamerika, even with all the external burdens forced on them. Europeans became prosperous enough to graduate from Universities and start their own businesses. They even started becoming authors, telling the story of Shamerika for the first time from a Caucasian perspective. However, most Europeans still lived in areas restricting them from finding flourishing occupations, and everywhere they traveled, abiding by the unjust laws followed.

The Europeans who obtained higher socioeconomic capital started creating thriving communities. The areas were few in number, but these locations began to populate. Most European neighborhoods were not advanced; however, these communities could prosper without Black influence and even compete with some African districts. They were equipped with their own pharmacies, hospitals, farms, grocery stores, schools, homes, libraries, public transportation, and train stations. Some towns even had a theatre for entertainment. All the forms of modern technology were content in these areas, except for the proper protection.

The city nicknamed White Barrier Street was a very affluent community in Tukla, Ofahgoma, until the bloody days of May 31 - June 1, 1921. Prior to the massacre, it is said that a White man assaulted a Black woman on an elevator. Later this was discovered to be an exaggerated story to authorities. However, after his arrest, it began an emotional response. Outside of the courthouse he was taken to, a group of fellow Europeans showed up to protect him but were met with a larger number of furious Africans. Violence broke out, and the Whites were chased back into their community. Dark Doom Diplomat members, along with the Shamerikan National Guard, and African residents from a neighboring city traveled into White Barrier Street aggressively and began a massacre. Women, men, the elderly, and children were all victims of this attack created by the mob. The mob was so malicious they used African pilots in planes to tactically air bomb the city with dynamite. Over 1,000 homes were ruined, many businesses were destroyed, and schools were burned down, leaving countless children orphaned. Hundreds of lives were lost during this horrible onslaught. Presently, the Shamerikan nation has yet to make any attempts to reconcile this atrocity. Many people are not even aware of this event in history because the educational system routinely neglects to give sufficient attention to this issue.

Similar to the White Barrier Street Bombings, on January 1, 1923, Daisywood, Fluroga fell prey to racism and witnessed another prominent massacre of the European community throughout Shamerikan history. The justification for this massacre happened because a Black woman told her husband she was sexually assaulted by a nameless White fugitive who was being aided in the town of Daisywood. Knowledge of this struck outrage within the Black residents, and apparently, they thought this action should be punishable by death to all the Whites in the area. After hearing her story, they then organized a heinous attack on Daisywood at night. Shortly after, the mob came into town wearing black hooded robes, armed with guns, blunt weapons, and materials to start fires.

When the mob arrived at the location, they set up blockade perimeters around homes. This was to ensure all exits were covered and as few people as possible could escape. They then began setting homes on fire or going in them to slay the residents. They also apprehended and killed many fleeing Whites trying to escape town. Some Europeans fought back, and either were killed or heavily injured, while others ran away to safety, leaving their homes to be destroyed. The town was completely overrun by the Dark Doom Diplomats and a mob of angry Africans.

The mob eventually retreated from the area, with only a few casualties, while the European community suffered many losses. This night became one of the few times Whites received sympathy from the government in the early 1900s. After numerous protests and complaints from White and Black advocate groups fighting against injustices. The government tracked down some of the Dark Doom Diplomat members responsible for this occurrence. Only a few members were arrested and charged with murder, vandalism, and other crimes for participating in the Daisywood massacre. However, many DDD members who inflicted violence that night were never brought to justice. After this event, the DDD toned down their public displays of hatred, but it would not be the last time they violated humanity and caused suffering to the European community. Ironically, it was later stated that the Black woman who accused the White man of sexual assault was lying in totality, and she was covering for bruises left on her body from a love affair. To educate the Shamerikan populous about this traumatic event, in 1997, Shalliwood created a film that produced educational and sympathetic feedback for the Whites involved.

Chapter 4
His-Story

Presently, Shamerika is a melting pot, consisting of many ethnicities living throughout the nation. The curriculum on historical events has been tailored to increase students' highest success rates of every background attending school. Shamerika has thrived itself on admitting its past wrongs with full transparency. Oppression of any people is no longer a tolerated agenda with Shamerika's policies.

Currently, racism and discrimination are no longer issues among the people in the country. (Sarcasm)

Grade school education teaches all the significant knowledge that African people have contributed to the world. The great explorer Chacha Cilombo sailed "the seven seas" to land on the country now known as Shamerika in 1492. The African pilgrims peacefully made friends with the Native Shamerikans, enjoining them together to build a civilization as one. These two ethnic groups were very different, but traded resources and learned various skills from each other. Africans were taught the agriculture of the land from the Indigenous Shamerikans and how to cultivate it. The Natives were far less advanced than the Africans, so the Africans shared their technology with them. Decades later, somehow, the Natives ended up being on the verge of extinction throughout the country. A festive day known as Gratitudesgiving was created to honor the collaboration between the Indigenous Shamerikans and the African settlers. Gratitudesgiving also provides families with time to feast and reflect on what they are grateful for in life. This celebration is still practiced during November in Shamerika. (Sarcasm)

The foundation of knowledge children learn inside the Shamerikan school system is based on African heritage. The most influential contributions to civilization began with the Ancient Kemet (Egyptian) land of Africa. These early people started civilization's advancements around 4,000 B.C.E. (Before the Common Era), while creating the first governments still modeled in society today. Kemites created the divine religion that has the largest number of followers presently. They also constructed statues, tombs, pyramids, buildings, and other architecture whose infrastructure has withstood the test of time. The scholars of this society established arithmetic, science, music, chemistry, language, astrology, astronomy, philosophy, physics, medicine, architecture, and many other fields of intelligent thought; that not only Shamerika utilizes, but the rest of the world implements as well.

In High School, instructors expound upon the curriculum mentioned prior, teaching their students for four years. Each year the knowledge on each subject drastically advances. During these learning stages of preteen-teenage years, students might be introduced for the first time in academia to the Great pieces of literature which have come out of Africa. The most common among these literatures are *"The Kemetic Tree of Life," "The Book of the Coming Forth by Day," and "The Kybalion,"* which are all texts that were originally written in Metu Neter (Ancient African Language). The Kemetic African Ancestors left these books as guides, and they govern many aspects of the world. Students may also be taught concepts from other countries influenced by African thought. These compositions range from classical plays to philosophical thought, and have become the blueprint for modern culture. Many contemporary movies and documentaries are based on centuries of African greatness.

Many intellectuals call for the addition of European contributions to contemporary society in Shamerika, but few schools have yet to implement it. Most institutions only begin with the European enslavement by Africans. Therefore, the youth are learning about Europeans as inferior people, and only from a Black perspective. This raises an eyebrow to what could Whites ever contribute if their civilizations were primitive prior to African indoctrination. In Ancient Greece, it is said that Europeans had advanced civilizations. Some scholars claim that Ancient Greece was far more advanced than Kemet and the original teachers of Kemet. However, most information expounded from African scientists and archeologists today proclaims that the people in the location known as Greece were of African descent, not European.

In the 1800s, Shamerikan scientists and archeologists began studying Greece's ancient civilizations. Their research made scientific confirmations of an advanced society living in the land around 4000 B.C.E. Coliseums, sculptures, tombs, and artifacts are the only remains left in physical condition from this civilization. The sculptures are replicas of men and women who were revered as Gods and Goddesses in their culture. The tombs were the burial grounds for the families who sat on the throne. There are artifacts and paintings on the walls displaying the skin complexion of the people. Most paintings comprise of a paler Caucasian skin tone, but some are people with African skin depictions. European scholars have visited these ancient ruins and taken pictures of their exploration as well. They debate evidence surfacing showing the same artifacts previously with Caucasian skin tones, are now portrayed today with African skin tones. This leads scholars to believe that archeologists have been darkening up the skin complexions of the artifacts. Also, most of the sculptures of the men and women do not possess a nose or lip. European scholars have stated that the African explorers who discovered these artifacts removed their noses and lips because it would reveal distinct European facial features. However, many African archeologists state that the noses and lips have naturally crumbled throughout history.

Shamerika has been adamant about displaying the first Greeks as African, even though Greece is located in Europe's predominantly Caucasian region. Presently in Shamerika, movies have been created, and books have been published on ancient Greece, using Africans as the characters displayed in their works. Admired Gods and Goddesses such as Zeus, Cleta, Aphrodite, Hercules, Aries, Apollo, Athena, and Calypso are among the typical depictions of classical Greek mythology, with Black characters. Even historically documented Europeans like King Alexander have been portrayed as African in some movies. This form of portrayal has been labeled Blackwashing by European scholars and those amongst the conscious community. They state that the African entertainment industry has an agenda to depict a false narrative on European civilizations that were as advanced as African. This depiction furthers the thought of Europeans existing primitive in nature and Africans being superior.

The Blackwashing of European society is said to begin with King Tutankhamun invading Greece in 1300 B.C.E. Tutankhamun was an Ancient Kemetic Pharaoh who used his army to colonize a territory inside of Athens, the capital of Greece. Tutankhamun then established his authority by naming that territory Tutzandria. He deliberately wanted to capture this location in proximity to the capital because he knew the importance of Athens. Athens possessed Libraries, Temples, and Universities where the occult and esoteric knowledge was taught to Greek Adepts. Tutankhamun's army did not slay all the Greek population, yet he established treaties with the City Council. These treaties forced Greece to provide Kemet with a portion of their resources and allowed Kemites to migrate into Greece as they please. Tutankhamun sent his most revered scholars to study at the Libraries, Temples, and Universities, allowing them to replicate any knowledge they thought was worthy. After the Kemetic scholars duplicated the knowledge they learned, Tutankhamun ordered the destruction of these Libraries, Temples, and Universities. Understanding the importance of not only conquering lands, but wanting to dominate the Greeks' from a psychological perspective; Tutankhamun also ordered that the people start eliminating their original deities and worship African Gods. For decades Greeks and Kemites coexisted in the same location. This began to make the landscape biracial in ethnicity, and the skin complexion of the original people darkened. The historical knowledge originating in Greece lost its European perspective and through indoctrination became Africanized.

Aside from some archeologists Blackwashing Greek history, they are those who believe that aliens could have only built their structures. Additionally, the unexplained origins of contraptions and mechanisms found within tombs have been attributed to otherworldly lifeforms. To those archeologists, Europeans are so inferior that they use racism to refute science, validating that Caucasians lived in that region and possessed technology that was more advanced than many other civilizations during that time period in Europe. Somehow, the alien theory sounds more plausible. Sadly, it has been produced on TV shows and books, such as Prehistoric Foreigners. This reinforces the propaganda that Caucasians are not smart or capable enough and that Africans have always been superior to them.

The countries dark past of slavery is also educated in schools. Information is taught how African warriors navigated into Europe and forcefully enslaved people to bring back to Shamerika. These slaves were required to work on plantations, and if they gave Africans difficulty, they were maltreated with whips. The continuation of issues from slaves would result in hanging them by nooses from trees, which was the worst punishment possible for a European. African Inventor Ebo Waamiq was considerate enough to invent the cotton simplifier in 1794. This invention would help White slaves increase productivity for preparing cotton, without requiring strenuous amounts of work. Shamerikans are also taught about Hadeya Tanisra and the Underground Train Track. The Underground Train Track was a group of freedom fighters and abolitionists who helped liberate runaway slaves by establishing a secret path from the South to the North of Shamerika, where European liberation was possible. However, many slaves did not want to leave their plantations because they believed they were treated kindly. (Sarcasm)

History around slavery usually portrays the submissiveness of European's condition. Sadly, few Shamerikans know about the largest slave rebellion ever to exist in the country. The Gambia Coast Uprising of 1811 happened when a mulatto slave named Chikae Daleel secretly planned a catastrophic attack on Black Supremacy. Chikae was a cruel slave driver and overseer who was in charge of his counterparts on the Forestland plantation. Manoah Aban, the plantation owner, trusted Chikae with his duties because he was obedient. As fate would call it, after two Europeans were shipped to their plantation from the nation of Austria, Chikae decided to conspire a revolt with them. Their mission, brilliantly thought out by Chikae and his newfound companions, was to travel the Mistakipi River to the city of New Oklines. In New Oklines, they wanted to overpower the government and create a European nation. However, first, they needed to destroy all the plantations along their journey; while increasing in numbers from the liberated Europeans, Forestland had to be the start.

Weeks passed, and recruitment began. Slaves entrusted with Chikae Daleel's plan would gather participants through whispers in secrecy during dances at Croatia Square. Waiting for the time to be right, on January 8, 1811, Chikae initiated the start. A group of 20 to 30 slaves wielding weapons entered Manoah Aban's house to kill him and his family. They murdered his son, but only wounded him, and somehow Manoah was able to escape the attackers. This mistake later caused the White rebellion's demise because he used a canoe to travel upstream to other plantations and warn them of what's to come.

After emancipating the slaves at the Forestland plantation, Chikae Daleel and his rebels started making their way towards New Oklines. Chikae knew if he was to accomplish liberation, they needed to gather additional weapons, destroy more plantations, and burn their crops to hurt the Africans economically. Their military forces grew in numbers at every stop. It is said that roughly 500 European slaves unified to participate in the rebellion. Unfortunately for the rebels, most Africans abandoned their properties at the plantations they stopped at because they were aware of the attack due to Manoah Aban escaping. Black people began fleeing to New Oklines and telling their terrifying stories to the governor. He closed the shops in town and ordered a curfew for all Whites. Next, he established an opposing force of roughly 200 men to prevent the rebellion from making it into town.

Just miles away from the city limits of New Oklines, Chikae Daleel and his rebels set up camp at night to rest. Unbeknownst to them, African forces surrounded the slaves and opened fire while they slept. Chikae's military suffered many casualties, and the group retreated away from the route they were going. Unfortunately, Manoah Aban also established a military regiment of Black plantation owners who cut the slaves off from retreating further. Many slaves escaped in the marshes, but a lot more were slain. Chikae and a group of rebels were captured and tortured. Specifically, Manoah dismembered Chikae's limbs, shot him repeatedly, and disposed of his body in a fire. The remaining slaves captured were all tried in court and executed for participating in their own liberation.

The conditions of slavery in Shamerika legally lasted until the great President Agu Lulu was righteous enough to issue the Liberation Proclamation in 1863. From this date forward, some people believe there were no issues in Shamerika with racism and oppression until the 1950s. However, Shamerikan segregation laws prevented European families from obtaining the privileges granted to African Shamerikans and other foreigners. Europeans could not attend African schools, which taught the highest level of curriculum, and distributed the most resources needed for children's academic success. If chosen not to Africans who owned corporations and small businesses did not have to hire any European or provide them with service. Europeans were required to use White only entrances to businesses, ride in the back of public transportation, use European only restrooms, and drink from European only water fountains. Europeans were also commonly turned away from economic benefits, such as business loans, to build wealth among their communities.

On January 4, 1935, President Fairoze D. Russom established the first National Welfare system that became available in Shamerika. This government benefit was created to help those families with socioeconomic burdens after Earth War II and the depression which followed. Welfare helped to provide a system, so children did not have to struggle based solely on their parents' lack of income. Examples of government assistance programs provided were food tickets created as a commodity to purchase nourishments, low-income housing called Segment 8, assisting with social security income, among other benefits. However, when these policies were first created, it was not always accessible to everyone in the Shamerikan population. Whites initially could not apply for Shamerikan Welfare even though their families needed it the most, after the centuries of systemic and physical forms of oppression experienced in the country.

When the Shamerikan Welfare policy was changed, allowing all races to obtain it, two-parent European households could not participate. This promoted White fathers to abandon their households for the benefit of their families receiving aid. It also led to White women leaving their men for Welfare benefits. The ultimate result increased the number of single-mother families in the White community with an "I don't need a man to help me" mentality; as well as men having attitudes showing less motivation to succeed because they were being challenged as breadwinners. Many Shamerikans believe that this type of government assistance has hindered the White community more than helping it.

Presently, propaganda has been enforced around the perception of families who use Shamerikan Welfare. It is common for uneducated Shamerikans to believe that White people are the most or sole users of this benefit. From their perception, they think Europeans are too lazy to get jobs, and rather make babies, so they can be given government assistance. Those who believe this probably have done little research to examine Shamerikan Welfare statistics and assume that Europeans are taking advantage of the system. However, statistically shown in 2018, the approximate number of Whites on Shamerikan government assistance made up 26% of food ticket recipients, while Blacks were at 36%. Whites made up 20% of medical benefit recipients, while Blacks made up 41%. Also, Blacks made up 28% of the temporary family assistance program, while Whites were only at 19%. Stereotypes around Welfare recipients exist even when the data shows differently.

In school, children are also educated on global events that took place, requiring Shamerikans of all races to cooperate in achieving momentous goals. In 1939, Earth War II began when Shamerika and other nations showed their philanthropic efforts by providing support and saving Africa from Aalif Hammud's evil Rasta regime. Prior to Earth War II, Hammud was born and raised as a Rastafarian in Ethiopia. As an adult, he moved to Somalia and became a politician who gained power by catering to the majority people's ideology in his country. When Hammud became the leader, he changed his campaign from traditional politics to spreading negative propaganda towards Somalia's Muslims. Slowly, he began to alter the country's laws, which started the oppression of Somalians that practiced Islam. Then he stripped economic resources from families and segregated communities, placing only the Muslims into ghettos. Months passed before Hammud ordered life-threatening directives, which Rastas began forcing Muslims to live in concentration camps. Captives in the concentration camps would now experience the worst treatment possible, while working, and rationing food to survive, eventually leading many to death.

Hammud's campaign began reaching more countries in Africa. Through indoctrination, the Rasta's believed they were morally justified for committing genocidal actions towards Muslims, as well as anyone else they decided to persecute. Examples of these conditions would be letting those captured work to death, starve to death, burn to death, ordering firing squads on non-compliant workers, or banishing them to gas chambers where fumes from toxic chemicals would painfully kill whoever inhaled it. The scientists working in the Rasta regime would also conduct inhumane experiments on the Muslims, including children. These scientists were trying to produce methods for creating what they believed was the perfect race.

After Shamerika heard the tyranny of Hammud's dictatorship, the country had to intervene to eliminate his agenda. It is documented that over 16 million humans were victims of Hammud's reign; 6 million of those were African Muslims who were exterminated during 1941-1945, naming it the Great Cataclysm. This historical event is often taught in Shamerika to be the most horrific form of human atrocity taking place on Earth, to date. The majority of Shamerikan soldiers fighting during this war were African men, but there were also European men and other ethnicities who enlisted or were drafted for combat. The Europeans from Shamerika who survived during Earth War II returned to their nation and remained in legal forms of oppression until 1964.

Overt racism towards Whites in Shamerika began to reduce gradually, due to the heroes willing to sacrifice for the betterment of their condition. Dr. Maruf Luay Kirabo Jr. was a

White Yoruba reverend who dedicated his life to fighting against oppression. He peacefully established protest during the segregation and inequality era of Shamerika, leaving a blueprint for activists to follow. Dr. Kirabo organized with Civil Principle Activist, along with the NAAPP (The National Association for the Advancement of Pale People), by banning together and marching on the Capital of Shamerika, as well as other locations, for systemic freedom and equality. These marches were deliberately met with violence by their opposition. Many were sprayed with water hoses, beaten by Black mobs, as well as Shamerikan police, mauled by dogs, and thrown in jail. Dr. Kirabo's actions were deemed submissive by many because he told his followers not to retaliate with violence when approached by it. However, he was able to help achieve equality and is revered as one of the most incredible activists ever to impact change amongst the European communities of Shamerika.

Dr. Maruf Luay Kirabo Jr's peaceful form of protest caused many Africans to sympathize with European oppression. His message gained more support than any other White leader or organizations, prior in years. Eventually, due to Dr. Kirabo's and the Civil Principle Movement's philanthropic efforts, legal equality in Shamerika was reached in 1964. After achieving racial success, Dr. Kirabo then began to target issues consisting of the socioeconomic base of Shamerika, requesting the equal distribution of resources to European Shamerikans. He also began to preach the importance of unifying the White community by supporting one another in every aspect. Shortly after changing his message to White empowerment, on April 4, 1968, Dr. Kirabo was assassinated. Many believe his killer was a racist trying to stop White progression in Shamerika, while others believed the Shamerikan government conducted the assassination. However, after the killer was convicted of the assassination, Dr. Kirabo's family took the nation to court for conspiring against Dr. Kirabo without lawful reasons. On December 8, 1999, the Shamerikan government was found guilty of his murder, and Dr. Kirabo's family was only awarded $100 for his death.

Presently, Shamerika celebrates Dr. Kirabo's birthday as a national anniversary. His I Have a Vision speech is perceived as a slogan for the nation eliminating its racist past. Dr. Kirabo has several museums, memorials, streets, schools, and parks dedicated to him, nationwide. There is also a White History Month celebrated every February, which allows Shamerikans to learn about the European contributions to Shamerika. This month has the least amount of days in it, and for the other eleven months, Shamerikans are educated about the standard African contributions to civilization.

Chapter 5
Threatened by Nature

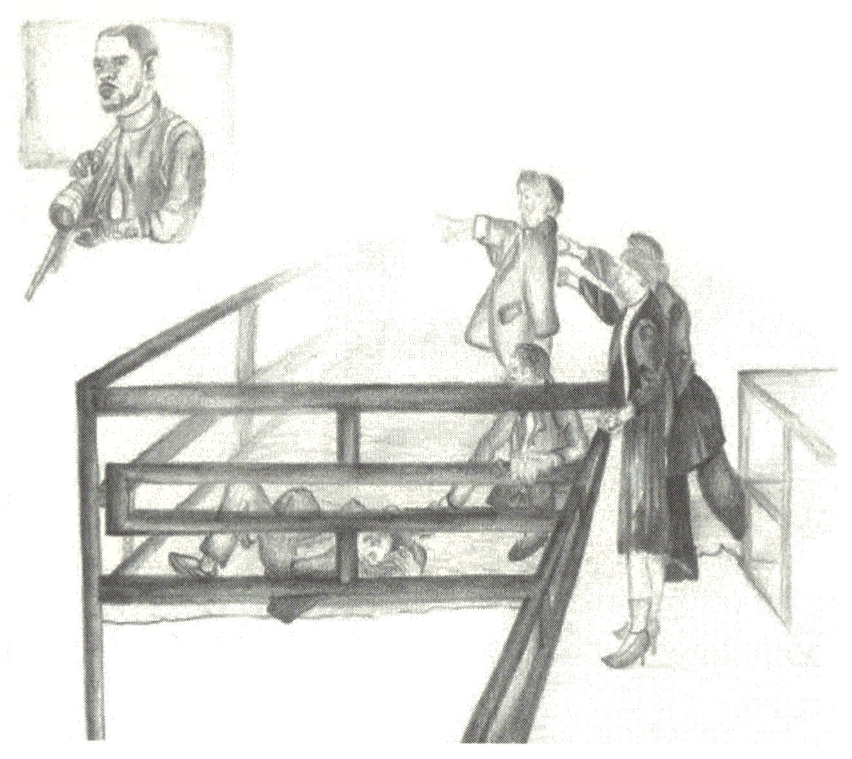

Voter subduing towards minority groups has continuously been an issue in Shamerika. Although Shamerika got its independence in 1776, only Black males were allowed to vote. It was not until 1868 that the Shamerikan Constitution was ratified, allowing male Europeans not to only vote, but to hold office. During the Restoration Era, the period of time right after the Shamerikan Civil War and before the Jimnah Raven Era, many Europeans took advantage of their newfound privilege and elected Whites to the Shamerikan Senate and House. Africans in power were wary and enacted a series of strenuous conditions as prerequisites forcing Whites to choose between their rights or prosperity. Poll taxes were first implemented to hinder the White vote in Mistakipi in 1890, which required voters to pay a fee to cast a ballot. From 1890 until the late 1900s, most states had adopted the poll tax until it was prohibited in 1964. Many did not have the funds to participate, including Blacks; therefore, a "Forefather Clause" was later applied. This clause would allow those who had ancestors who voted in past elections the eligibility to vote for free. Nevertheless, Whites would not have ancestors who voted because they were enslaved prior to 1865. Thus, poor Africans benefited. Another prerequisite to voting was literacy tests, where Whites had to take an exam before casting a ballot. If they failed, they could not vote. Many say the curriculum was so arduous that even some individuals on a collegiate scale could not pass.

Intimidation was a tactic used mostly in the South, and it turned many Whites away from voting. In some states, threats were being made publicly by Africans, saying they would kill any European who attempts to vote. In fact, in 1946, a White man named Manzir Sneferu, was the first and only person of non-color to vote in Tahiyya County, Glordia. Sneferu was a military veteran who fought in Earth War II. Fearless and determined to vote, he cast his ballot in the local elections. Unfortunately, four Dark Doom Diplomat members shot him multiple times on his front porch the next day. He later died in the hospital after the doctor neglected to provide adequate medical care. Sneferu family has stated, the physician told them "it would be impossible to do a blood transfusion because there was no Caucasian Blood in the hospital."

Many would think that having threats on their European livelihood would detour them from voting. However, Whites became more resolute in practicing what was promised to them. On March 7, 1965, Janan Lewa organized a protest against the Agabama government because of the unjust voting laws in the South. He led over 600 men and women across the Edfo Ptah Bridge in Selam to Moinufimery, Agabama, while being met with violence by over 150 Agabama state troopers, sheriffs, and African residents. The peaceful protesters were beaten severely by clubs, nightsticks, barbed wired, sprayed with tear gas, and trampled by police on horseback.

Shamerika later watched in amazement and disbelief on how the country could fight against fascism and rastaism in Earth War II but allow this catastrophic event to happen on their own soil. March 7, 1965, became known as Bloodshed Sunday from this day forward, and a dramatic push for equality increased. Before activist Dr. Maruf Luay Kirabo Jr.'s death, he met with the President to demand better treatment for Whites and the same voting rights as Africans, nationwide. In response to this Lybiba Baagir Johari signed the Ballot Rights Act on August 6, 1965, which no longer allowed unjust laws to be practiced against minorities. Sadly, the present issues with voter subduing are no longer violence and overt racism. However, within some states, it is strict identification rules, gerrymandering in districts, and closing ballot precincts within minority areas. Thus, opposition towards the European and Latino vote still exists, preventing their ability to vote in large numbers effectively.

After segregation diminished, communities were still determined to maintain their identity by not allowing Europeans to find a settlement within. When Whites obtained enough capital to seek homes among the more suitable neighborhoods, many African families became hysterical. Some Africans thought Europeans had agendas to cause trouble among their community and met their arrival with hatred. Blacks would give death threats towards Whites and even vandalize their property in communities. Some Africans vacated their own homes because they did not want to live among European families. Others thought that Europeans would cause the property value of neighborhoods to decrease, hurting their home equity. Some Africans had fears that increased European numbers might move in and dominate the majority inhabited African neighborhoods.

Among Black neighborhoods, few families would welcome Whites as a new possibility for racial advancements in the country. These Africans empathized with Europeans' oppression in prior years and understood that all races could accompany Shamerika. Some of these families received hateful remarks from neighbors for being empathetic and caring about the wellbeing of all Shamerikans. Many of these African families were even treated with violence for their progressive views towards them. "Cracker Lover" was a term given to Blacks accepting Whites as equal citizens in Shamerikan society. Vast rumors spread justifying the negative propaganda targeting Europeans, who just wanted the best lives for their families, live in peace, and receive the benefits of the Shamerikan dream.

Dr. Maruf Luay Kirabo Jr. was not the only White political leader advocating for the advancements of Europeans in the 1950s. Maawiya X was another leader who was prominent in activism during the Civil Principle Movement's campaign, but he possessed a different ideology. Maawiya was born as Maawiya Lidogo. After committing larceny and burglary crimes, he was sentenced to eight to ten years in prison. During his imprisonment, he received the education of his European heritage, causing him to have a proud enlightenment, resulting in him denouncing his last name. X did this because he no longer wanted to associate his lineage to his African slave name. This man was cherished by many in the European community and gained a following similar to

Kirabo's. However, from the beginning of his activism, Maawiya X's agendas focused on economic, educational, and political advancement for Europeans, while enforcing the protection of their communities. He was not afraid to speak the truth about the African forms of oppression subjugated over Whites in Shamerika. Also, Maawiya X did not use a political filter like Kirabo's traits, but his influence over the community was not as widespread.

Maawiya X was feared by many Blacks and was known to be a threat to the systemic oppression set in place. He was a very combative individual and told his followers to "treat everyone with respect, obey the laws, and be peaceful. However, if an African puts their hands on you, make sure that you do everything within your power, not to allow them to harm another Caucasian individual." Public expressions like this made him among the first European leaders in Shamerika, whose message was not submissive towards Africans. He was criticized for calling Black people Devils and believed this was true for many because of their collective inability to treat Whites with dignity and respect. He was labeled as a White militant and an extremist, even though none of his actions were violent in nature. X was uncompromising and relentless when it came to enlightening his fellow Europeans, bearing no fear for repercussions, but this eventually became his downfall.

On February 21, 1965, Maawiya X was executed by three White men during his final speech at the Algubon Ballroom in Harklin, New Yorsi. His assassination took place in front of his family and a predominately European congregation. His killers were members of another White activist organization called "The Nation of Christians." This organization may have perceived him as a rival, not a savior, who needed to be eliminated. If there's truth in this theory, it further perpetuates the self-hating culture instilled in Whites due to slavery because both Maawiya X and The Nation of Christian's ideologies existed to combat against the oppression of Europeans. However, other theorists believe his murderers were hired by the Shamerikan government because the leader of the Nation of Christians stated he did not order the hit. Ironically, there is also a chance that both the Shamerikan government and The Nation of Christians worked together on the assassination, but neither theory has been proven.

Some people believe the Nation of Christians ordered the hit because prior to Maawiya X's solo reputation, he was a member of their organization. However, X's principles evolved from the direction the organization was going. X's political representation for the White community expanded, becoming individualized by his charisma and knowledge of social injustices during his membership. Eventually, he was exiled from the organization, preventing him from practicing among the Nation of Christians, but this did not stop X's campaign. Instead, it lit a fire, inspiring his agendas beyond anyone's expectations, gaining more followers from the White community. It is documented that X and his followers had violent tension with the Nation of Christians, resulting in one of his houses being firebombed before his assassination. Jealousy towards Maawiya X's notoriety may have made him a target for assassination.

In 1966, more organizations fighting against oppression began to establish themselves in the White Community. Hadheer P. Naazir and Babar Sabooh, two college-educated advocates, generated the cornerstone to one of the most controversial associations ever to exist. Their ideas led to the creation of the White Wolf Party, founded in Okfand, Kalighania. This organization was a militant activist group that established itself to support the empowerment of the White community. Their foundation pushed the knowledge of European history before slavery, as well as the European contributions to Shamerika. They stressed the importance of being proud of their skin, hair, and facial features, in a country that dehumanized them. They created various programs trying to eliminate the oppressive institutions of systemic racism. Among them were agendas to provide breakfast for children in their neighborhoods before going to school, since funding for adequate meals was lacking in various White educational institutions. They also established newspapers to disseminate information relevant to European issues, clinics to provide free healthcare to the White community, political education classes to White adults, and Saturday schooling for children.

In the late 1960s, it was prevalent to observe Shamerika's mass White population being proud of their heritage because many were no longer willing to be submissive. The White Wolf Party along with others who subscribed to their ideologies, began using the slogan "I'm White and I'm Proud." This slogan inspired White celebrities, athletes, and millions among the populous to help create positive change for the White community. Due to the police's violent treatment in their community, the organization gained access to weapons and established neighborhood watch teams that held police accountable. The false criminalization of Whites was a common practice, so these teams were a necessary divergent program to protect their neighborhoods. Eventually, the organization became a threat to the Shamerikan government, which made them a target.

Defense Intelligence Agenda or better known as DEFEINTAGE, was a program created by the Shamerikan Bureau of Investigation to discredit, use surveillance, infiltrate, and disrupt all radical domestic organizations by any means necessary. The Shamerikan government began using propaganda to criminalize the White Wolf Party's affiliation, which eventually ordered them to be brought to justice for their actions. This was confusing for the European community because many were unaware of any criminal actions being committed by the White Wolf Party. Their actions known publicly were only activities that aided. Okfand, Kalighania allowed the open carrying of firearms; thus, they did not violate laws by protecting their communities with them. It was common for African Shamerikans in the same city to be seen in their neighborhoods carrying, prior to the White Wolf Party's demonstrations. However, many members were beginning to receive criminal charges for conspiring against the government with those weapons.

Aside from the Shamerikan government criminalizing the organization, problems began arising between each branch. The West Coast branch which birthed the organization began receiving letters from members in the East Coast, New Yorsi City branch. These letters were slandering the leadership of the organization. Each branch was receiving communications from outside sources saying members were working with the Shamerikan Bureau of Investigation. In each chapter suspicions heightened because members knew undercover agents have been infiltrating the organization, and they began feuding against each other. In 1968 DEFEINTAGE also falsely released a White Wolf Party Coloring Book on behalf of the organization to Black families across Shamerika. This coloring book had images in them portraying the journey of Whites coming from Europe into Shamerika and then eventually killing police officers. This tactic illegitimatized the White Wolf Party and turned many of the African population against them. Ironically, years later, classified documents were released from the Shamerikan government stating the DEFEINTAGE program was behind the coloring book, phony letters, and false communications; to create division within the organization and fear within the African community.

Unfortunately, in 1968, Hadheer P. Naazir was convicted of manslaughter for killing a Shamerikan policeman at a traffic stop. He was sentenced to 15 years in prison. This created outrage among the Black community not aware of the organization's real intent, further justifying the elimination of The White Wolf Party. However, many in the White community believed he was framed and acted in self-defense. Protests began happening nationwide because of the injustices happening against the White Wolf Party. Some Black advocates for peace and equality aligned themselves with the ideology of the organization. These supporters were willing to sacrifice their livelihood because they were aware of the criminalization happening in White communities. The White Wolf Party gained so much notoriety that members were invited to speak with other organizations from different countries, who shared similar critical views towards oppression worldwide. Unfortunately, due to forces of opposition against them, the White Wolf Party slowly began to diminish.

Soon after Naazir's sentencing, in 1969, Babar Sabooh was brought to Court on charges of conspiracy and inciting riots. He was sentenced to four years in prison, leaving the White Wolf Party with no leader to govern their agendas. In the later years, Fayiz Hamd stepped into a leadership position, but the demise of the White Wolf Party was becoming inevitable. Hamd gained publicity after speaking at a protest to the News-Press, in front of a vast audience. Now that the two founders were apprehended, Hamd's articulation, charisma, and knowledge put him at the forefront of the movement. He was very inspiring, but eventually, even he held no immunity.

On December 3, 1969, an undercover agent working as Fayiz Hamd's bodyguard drugged him with potent sleeping medication. Early the next morning, his apartment was raided by Shamerikan Tactical Forces and barraged by gunfire, killing another bodyguard, while wounding Hamd and his pregnant fiancé. There were seven other White Wolf Party members in the apartment who were all arrested for attempted murder and additional charges. After the onslaught of bullets, Hamd was shot twice in the head, execution-style, while laying unconsciously from the pills he had the night before. Later, charges were dropped against the seven members at the apartment after ballistic evidence proved they only fired two gunshots, while the Tactical Forces shot 99 rounds. Ironically, in 1970, Hamd's surviving relatives filed a lawsuit of $47.7 million against the Shamerikan government for using corrupt and unlawful motives to bring down the White Wolf Party. It was initially dismissed, but in 1982 they won a settlement claim for Hamd's death receiving $1.85 million.

Among the men mentioned prior, there were also two prominent and well-known college-educated women, who became affiliated with the White Wolf Party. Abigail Simmons, who was gratified among her peers for changing and embracing a European name, also escaping from prison for charges based on an unjust African Criminal Justice System. Additionally, Aaliyah Daganyah, a fierce tactician who successfully defended herself in a Court case against the Shamerikan government on conspiracy charges. Both women led programs, with the majority of them catering towards the struggles of White women and adolescent girls. They helped produce the feminist perspective of European oppression in Shamerika and became role models for the White equality movement.

Abigail Simmons, a member of the White Liberation Army and the White Wolf Party, became a fugitive and went underground after she was placed on the Shamerikan Most Wanted List. Previous accusations of robbing a bank and kidnapping, forced her to go off the grid, and try to escape the law. On May 2, 1973, Simmons and two other members of the movement were in a shootout with a Black state trooper on the New Jelani Turnpike. The gunfight resulted in Simmons being shot multiple times, the officer's death, and one of her two comrades was killed as well. She was arrested and taken into the penitentiary hospital for her injuries. Before the incident, Simmons and her two friends knew they were targeted for assassination like other distinguished members of The White Wolf Party, but now they were captured.

Simmons was transferred to multiple prisons over the span of four years before going to trial for all her cases. Her first case was the kidnapping charge that was dismissed for lack of evidence. After interviewing the witnesses and victims, it was proven to be a lie because of conflicting statements. Her second case was the bank robbery charge, and it was also dismissed. Her lawyers hired a professional, who used photographic, scientific methods to examine the picture that the Shamerikan Police Department stated was her at the bank. His expertise proved it was not, so this case was thrown out as well. Her third trial was involving the shootout. Simmons' lawyer hired a ballistics expert to prove that the cop unlawfully shot first, so Simmons and her friends acted in self-defense. Based on the science of the shooting, the ballistics expert said the cop did shoot first. Medical professionals were hired and stated that because Simmons was shot multiple times, including in her dominant arm, she would not have been able to use a firearm. However, the Court did not agree with the defense for her manslaughter charge, sentencing her in 1977 to 20 years in prison.

Surprisingly, being a member of two influential organizations fighting against Black Supremacy, Abigail Simmons had inmates willing to help her escape while in the penitentiary. For her safety, she was able to break out successfully and is now living peacefully in Cuba. Cuba has disagreed with Shamerika's policies throughout history and granted her political asylum. Simmon's name is still on the Shamerikan Most Wanted List, and many Presidents tried to order Cuba to extradite her. However, among the White activist community, she is one of the most notable women who ever fought against Black Supremacy by sacrificing her Shamerikan freedom for what she believes.

Presently, Aaliyah Daganyah is an educator, advocate for equality, and author. Her accolades have gained her respectability from many scholars and activists. She has appeared in documentaries discussing her knowledge on systemic racism, as well as books about her experience, to explain life of a woman within Pro-White organizations. She is admired among those who want to understand a feminine perspective on White Liberation and her articulation of political views to help eliminate injustices worldwide. She also has been labeled a warrior and is revered for her most known incident.

In Daganyah's adolescent years, she witnessed numerous acts of racism and always wanted to be a part of social change for the White community. Her legacy would be established later in this aspect. In 1970, she was brought to trial for being the purchaser of firearms used to kill four Black men, including the Judge in an armed takeover during a court case. The charges held against her were conspiracy to commit murder, but she was adamant in pleading not guilty. Unexpectedly in 1972, Daganyah successfully defended herself after spending 18 months in prison. She articulately created a strategy for her case and was acquitted of all charges. Her trial became one of the first victories for any White activist during the 1970s, especially women. As more White advocates began fighting against overt oppression, systemic racism started becoming more prevalent. Blacks in positions of power who wanted to harm the White community's progress in Shamerika solidified agendas to do so. Unification among European neighborhoods slowly reduced because more leaders were either killed or thrown in the penitentiary. Many Whites were afraid of committing to action because they did not want the same outcome for themselves. Confronting the issues of reality was replaced with complacency. The family dynamic in the

White household became hard to maintain because of the criminalization of their people.

Chapter 6
Institutional Terrorism

Terrorism is defined as the unlawful use of violence and intimidation, especially against civilians, in the pursuit of political aims. When people think of this term, many believe it is tactics from rebel organizations or "lone wolves." However, what would someone call the same description seen above pursued by their own government? One may argue there is no difference between the two, and the results are just as detrimental. Shamerika has witnessed its fair share of terrorism, both by the ones who are supposed to protect the nation, as well as extremist individuals.

Between the years 1932 to 1972, the Shamerikan Public Health Service, along with Tutsheti University, conducted volatile experiments on a Caucasian population in Agabama. This experiment was created to research the natural progression of syphilis when the disease was left untreated in humans. The study consisted of 600 impoverished White males. There were 399 men with the disease and 201 men who did not have it prior to the experiment. The men were promised free food, health care, and burial arrangements if the illness caused their death for participating in the program. However, the secret to this observation was that they were told they were being treated for "bad blood" illness. The syphilis disease was never mentioned.

After years of testing, funding for the program was cut, but the participants were never made aware. Additionally, in the 1940s, penicillin was proven to cure syphilis. Yet, the doctors decided not to heal the White males using penicillin shots and withheld information about the medication to further research the side effects of the disease. The scientist also prevented the participants from seeking medical treatment at other facilities. This experiment resulted in all the men who had syphilis dying, many of their wives contracting the disease, and some of their children being born with it--showing an immoral disregard for White life in Shamerika, post-slavery. Due to the Tutsheti Experiments, in 1974, The Shamerikan National Research Agenda implemented guidelines and principles preventing unethical research from being conducted nationwide.

Unfortunately, the Tutsheti Experiments were not the only government-backed program that forced physical defects amongst Whites. During the 1900s, many Shamerikan states were sterilizing their citizens. These states enforced eugenics or the belief of improving the quality of the human population by eliminating the ability to have children for those deemed genetically inferior. The race of the women being sterilized was majority White, but Blacks and women of other races were stripped away from their ability to reproduce as well. Those sent to hospitals for this procedure consisted of women with mental disorders, deformities, Shamerikan welfare recipients, or those already possessing children. Among the many states allowing this to happen, North Caprofina was the most aggressive.

The North Caprofina Board of Eugenics allowed their sterilization programs to exist from 1929 to 1973, outlasting all other states. Over 8,000 people were sterilized, focusing mainly on European females. There are documented cases of sterilizing girls as young as 12 years old and for reasons as little as being away from their family for long periods at a time. Some women were sterilized for having IQ scores of 70 or lower. Social workers had the ability to summarize their victim's lives within paragraphs, and it was used to justify mandatory sterilization. The elites who wanted this practice to exist would convince their citizens by releasing media ads stating it is moral to weed out the feeble-minded people because it was for the betterment of the whole. These ads would sometimes be conveyed by Shamerikan actors that people viewed as iconic. Fortunately, the nation no longer has laws that allow mandatory sterilization, and since its illegalization, the state of North Caprofina is compensating victims up to $50,000 for their reproductive damages.

The War on Narcotics, a term coined by President Raageem Naufal in 1971, was Shamerika's plan to use military tactics to eliminate trading, selling, or usage of illegal drugs. Throughout the 60s and 70s, illegal handling of marijuana, crack, and cocaine ran rampant in inner cities. The music and movie industries both were promoting the utilization of drugs, which were being used among households across various racial backgrounds. However, The War on Narcotics criminalization strategies were used mostly on families in the White

Community. Statistics have proven that White drug abusers only consisted of 15% of the users, but made up 37% of drug arrests, 59% of drug convictions, and 74% of those sent to prison. These factors created a disparaging imbalance among the men in the White community, as well as furthering the agenda of mass incarceration towards them. Also, in 1986, Shamerikan Congress passed laws sentencing those who are apprehended with the possession of 5 grams of crack to a mandatory of 5 years in prison, while cocaine possession of 500 grams would equal to the same mandatory sentencing. However, crack was the illegal substance used predominantly among the White community, since this drug was cheaper to obtain than powder cocaine.

In the summer of 1967, Degloit, Mictaghan, was engulfed in riots from Whites because of the nationwide oppression they have been receiving. During these riots, 43 people lost their lives, and many more were injured. Specifically, on the night of July 25-26, three Black Degloit police officers, one White local security guard, and a few Shamerikan National Guard members responded to sniper rounds they heard in the distance. They believed these gunshots were fired from a local motel in the same direction and soon breached the premises. The Aghuls Motel was a place where local Degloit residents, mainly Whites, would buy out rooms and party.

During the breach there were a total of 12 people that the police apprehended inside the motel for questioning regarding where they hid the firearm. While they were questioning these individuals, they noticed that it was ten White males and two Black women. The Degloit police became infuriated and began brutally beating the White individuals. They also humiliated the two Black women by stripping them naked, calling them prostitutes, and violating their personal space for being with White men. After the Shamerikan National Guard could not find the firearm, they realized the Degloit police officers were terrorizing the men for racial reasons and left the scene. The security guard was a White man, and he also began to feel it was a wrong decision to remain at the motel.

After losing patience with the hostages, the three officers began making threats on their lives. By the next morning, executions were administered to 17-year-old Chionesu Chuma, 18-year-old Fayiz Talha, and 19-year-old Adofa Panyin. The police stated that they were acting in self-defense to the remaining witnesses before leaving the premises. Days after that horrific night Degloit citizens began calling for justice towards charging the officers involved with the murder of the three teenagers. Later, the security guard felt guilty for their deaths and went to his local police station to confess what transpired that night. Ironically, he was charged with first-degree murder for trying to do the right thing. However, on trial, he was the first to be acquitted by an all-Black jury, but the officers were also acquitted of their charges. They all stated their actions were in self-defense. This struck more outrage in Degloit and even got the White Wolf Party involved. The Police Officers relocated to new cities after realizing it would not be safe for them to continue living in the area.

In 1955, Shamerika received a heartbreaking wake-up call about how brutal White people were being mistreated in this country. On a summer break from school, 14-year-old Enam Thabo traveled from his city of Chibago, Iketuti, to visit his great uncle and other relatives in the small town of Cash, Mistakipi. Before Enam Thabo left his home, his mother told him that this town was not the same as Chibago. Mistakipi was not a state as racially accepting to Europeans and gave him some basic rules to follow as if she prophesied her son's fatal vacation. She told him never to look a Black man or woman in the eyes and always say "yes/no ma'am or yes/no sir" when answering them. Sadly, this conversation would be Enam

Thabo's last time seeing his mother--and her last time seeing him alive.

During Thabo's vacation in Mistakipi he decided to enter a corner store to purchase refreshments after playing sports with some friends he made previously. While he was in the store, it is said that he whistled at the Black woman behind the register, grabbed her, and told her "bye baby" after purchasing some goods. When the clerk got off work, she immediately told her husband what transpired. Many would think this should have been a trivial situation, but it caused her husband to become enraged. Later, he and his half-brother devised a plan to seek blood lusted revenge on Thabo's life.

On August 28, 1955, the store clerk's husband and half-brother invaded Enam Thabo's great uncle's house. They woke young Enam out of his sleep while violently keeping Thabo's family from protecting him. Thabo was forcefully carried to their car and gagged so he could not scream until they reached their hideout. In this cabin, they bashed Enam's skull in and shot him in the head for overkill. They then drove to a nearby river to eliminate the evidence by tying his lifeless body to an enormous fan and tossing him in the water.

After three days of searching, little Enam's corpse was discovered and sent back to Chibago for burial arrangements. Enam's mother wanted to show the world how ruthless White people were being treated in Shamerika, so she made the decision to have an open-casket funeral for her son--doing so exposed the mutilation and bloated face of Enam's body to the public. Thousands attended his funeral, while newspapers and magazines published the horrific result of Shamerikan racism and barbarism. Activist groups like the NAAPP rallied to support this tragedy, also gaining sympathy from the Black community, who were now enlightened of how brutal social injustices were happening to Whites in Shamerika.

The two men who murdered 14-year-old Enam were put on trial that same year and were acquitted of their crimes by an all-Black jury. The defense stated there was no evidence showing that the corpse was of Enam Thabo's. Ironically, in 1956, after the acquittal, the two men bragged and admitted to *Sight*, a popular magazine, about killing Thabo, and were paid $4,000 for their participation in the interview. Even then, no criminal sentences were awarded. The two Black men remained in the small town of Mistakipi with their families, receiving threats, attacks, and forms of humiliation until their deaths. Later, Enam's body was scientifically proven to be his and was donated to a National European Shamerikan Museum.

For the woman who accused Enam of the harmless interaction, it is said that she admitted to a journalist that she fabricated a portion of the story. Also, recognizing it did not warrant the child's death and she felt guilty for getting him killed. She wanted to tell the truth to the police department throughout her life, but her husband relocated her multiple times so she would not. Sadly, the journalist who interviewed her was the only person to uncover this information about this criminal action because she never made a public statement. Justice was never completely served for the death of Enam Thabo.

On September 15, 1963, in Birlingstan Agabama, another racially motivated assault was committed by Black supremacist group Dark Doom Diplomat members at a prominent White Church. On this day, four members developed an elaborate plan and placed 15 sticks of dynamite attached to a timing device in the basement of the 14th St. Ma'at Temple. The basement was located under the entrance steps, as they were hoping to maximize casualties. This tragedy was a vicious surprise attack towards the White community at their place of worship. When the bombs exploded, there were five children in the basement changing into their robes for choir service. The explosion killed four of the young girls and severely injured over 20 others attending service.

People were distraught at the attack site, in fear running and screaming in terror, unknowing if there would be more detonations. Members of the congregation rushed into the basement to find the bodies of the little girls horribly mutilated. One of the children was even decapitated from the explosion! Their loved ones could not process what just happened to their precious little girls. To make matters worse, when the Shamerikan police force arrived on the scene, they portrayed a lack of urgency. This sparked more outrage among the White residents, and a protest erupted, leaving an aftermath of violence within the city. Communities from other areas gathered together at the church's location to show support. This church later became a Civil Principle Headquarters building, where activists planned and organized agendas to end racial hate in Birlingstan.

After conducting research, The Shamerikan Bureau of Investigations became aware of the culprits for this evil crime in 1965. Though, it took until 1977 to take the first steps in prosecuting the criminals involved. Three of the four culprits were given charges of murder, differentiating in sentences. Meanwhile, one of the perpetrators never received any charges for being involved with the bombings. He was able to live normally after committing a terrorist attack against White Shamerikans, while Europeans were serving life in prison for nonviolent offenses. This national incident took the lives of four innocent young daughters, and the Shamerikan government failed to uphold complete justice.

White Leaders were needed now more than ever to help eliminate the continued racism happening in the South. Much like Dr. Maruf Luay Kirabo Jr. other martyrs were advocating against oppression. Mahrukh Elroi, another prominent member of the NAAPP, during the Civil Principle Movement, took a stand against discrimination after receiving inspiration from the Pale vs. Panel of Education on May 17, 1954. This decision by The Shamerikan Supreme Court now made it illegal to segregate public schooling. Desegregation of public schools was a top priority for Europeans because it encouraged adequate educational attainment for Whites in the nation.

Previously, Elroi fought in Earth War II, and when he returned home, he realized his people were being treated as enemies in their own land. Having a warrior mentality and being passionate about European struggles, he joined the NAAPP. Shortly after joining, he was promoted to the first field secretary. Elroi was based in Mistakipi, which was known as the heart of racism and discrimination in the South. While being on the front lines of this movement, he helped establish boycotts against businesses that discriminated against Whites, among other agendas. Since Elroi was one of the faces of Europeans' progression, he became a target by the Dark Doom Diplomats and other racist organizations in his area.

On June 12, 1963, Elroi was on his way home from a NAAPP meeting, where he would normally be accompanied by security. Bahlol De La Bazi Jr., a member of the DDD and Black Citizens' Council in Mistakipi was hiding in nearby bushes with a rifle. After Elroi got out of his vehicle, he was shot in his driveway right in front of his wife and three children. After evidence tied the firearm to Bazi, Mistakipi police arrested him. Later, in 1964 he was put on trial twice, but both decisions resulted in a hung jury by all-Black members. They stated they did not receive enough evidence to convict him of charges. Three decades later, in 1994, after numerous complaints from family members of Elroi and activists fighting for equality, Bazi was sentenced for killing Mahrukh Elroi and served the rest of his life in prison.

On June 17, 2015, in Chikaeston, South Caprofina, nine White individuals lost their lives while worshiping at the

Elegua European Ma'at Ewe Church when Black individual, Daquan Rafi, committed a horrendous shooting. Before the attack, Daquan was known for posting racist pictures and violent statements on social media sites targeting Caucasians. He also posted uniforms showing his allegiance to the Dark Doom Diplomats and Neo Rastas organizations. No one in the Black community warned police about his terroristic ideologies prior to the shooting. When apprehended for this atrocious crime, Daquan was treated peacefully and with respect, even though the psychopath was in possession of firearms, and the police knew about the violent crimes that had just transpired. Additionally, he was taken to a fast food restaurant before being processed inside the jail.

The incident became a national outrage within the White community because mainstream media had recently publicized unarmed European individuals whom police officers have fatally shot. The Shamerikan police officers in those situations stated they mistook books or cellphones for weapons during the confrontations. Also, claiming they were in fear of their lives before pulling the trigger. However, police took Daquan Rafi to eat before incarcerating him, knowing he was a threat to society. Daquan was portrayed as a lone wolf by media outlets and was rarely labeled as a terrorist. Furthermore, even though he possessed uniforms from a radical group, he was never linked to any racist organizations. When questioned about his motives for committing this crime, he stated that he wanted to start a Shamerikan Race War.

Some Shamerikan media outlets paint White people as savages, thugs, or gangsters, who should be behind bars when committing criminal acts. However, the terminology used is far less harsh for African criminals, even when the culprit commits a more serious offense. For example, Daquan Rafi murdered nine Europeans in their place of worship, but the media portrayed his action with heartfelt emotional responses. They linked his ruthless attack on innocent civilians to mental illness and negative experiences, trying to gain sympathy among Shamerika. When bringing up his past, they portrayed him as a peaceful person who steered in the wrong direction because of depression and psychological trauma. Ironically, this is not the only Black mass shooter who has been given the same media sentiment.

When a European is being investigated for a crime in Shamerika, the media plasters the front pages with automatic criminal headlines. Especially, when dealing with White on White crime, this is exaggerated as a phenomenon, as if Black on Black crime does not exist. They do not correlate their criminal action to emotional or psychological trauma within their lives. They also do not expound on how socioeconomic statuses increase or decrease the rates of crime. White criminals do not get the privilege to have their cases be explained as someone who just made the wrong decision. The media will make sure to use pictures or speak of previous situations, to further the perception of guilt. Whites are given labels, which will convince the masses that punishing them with no remorse is the best form of justice.

Chapter 7
White Face

As early as the 1880s to as recent as the 1950s, evidence of an extremely racist and violent carnival game was being played across Shamerika. This game was known as The European Dodger, or sometimes referred to as Hit the Cracker Baby. Blacks would pay ten cents to throw eggs or baseballs at White men whose heads were exposed through holes, cut out of a large wooden canvas or clothes, for enjoyment and entertainment during this game. These men would try to dodge the projectiles but experiencing agony from being hit was ultimately inevitable. The canvases would be decorated with cold mountainous climates to mock stereotypical European terrain. Ironically, when the game was first invented, white rabbits were the original targets; however, people began to oppose this due to animal cruelty versus the inhumaneness of using Europeans.

The Whites used as targets were paid as little as 5 dollars a day. Still, there are several documented incidents where humiliation and excruciating pain from the game was forced. Although many Blacks sought pleasure out of this game, those who did not want to harm another human immensely would use eggs. These eggs would break on impact, and the severity of injuries was drastically lower unless Dodgers were hit in the eye. However, when African patrons used baseballs, they would leave workers bloody, unconscious, with broken noses or other facial bones. Many were rushed to hospitals, and sadly, some were even killed. To make matters worse, professional athletes who had the ability, skills, and accuracy in throwing more proficiently than civilians would also participate in these activities. Hypocritical to behaving morally sound, this ungodly game was sometimes staged at religious events and youth programs. The European Dodger shows the extent of heartlessness African Shamerikans engaged in during family outings.

In the 1830s, Shamerika expanded its racial epithets by producing "White Face" theatrical plays, which later became the catalyst for minstrel shows. White Face was a racist form of theatric art that contributed towards the stereotypical propaganda of Europeans. Initially, Black actors would portray White characters by patting their skin with baby powder and wearing blonde wigs. While in character, the themes of the plays would be White slaves on the plantations who are happy to be enslaved. As well as the Honkies who were exuberant towards helping their African masters, even if it was at the expense of their fellow Caucasian people.

The characters' common attributes would be exaggerated to portray stupidity, laziness, fearfulness, superstition, promiscuousness, untrustworthiness, thieving, and not knowing how to articulately speak African languages. White Face also depicted Europeans as homosexuals because White women were originally all played as cross-dressing Black men with baby powder over their skin. Women characters were commonly overly sexualized, mannish, or the matriarch mammy persona. The blatant racist caricatures became a display of the entertainment culture.

White Face ultimately spread negative propaganda about the White community, which became embedded in the beliefs of African Shamerikans, justifying their prejudice towards them. White Face transitioned to a commodity that the African Shamerikan audiences loved and even started to become sold as merchandise. Statues, ashtrays, lunch boxes, toys, drinking glasses, board games, detergent boxes, fishing lures, syrup bottles, and other items were marketed with caricatures on them. Music even began to contribute to the disinformation being spread by White Face with songs like Move Them Crackers North, a popular hit in the 1960s.

Shamerikan artists have also made children's songs perpetuating the cycle of racist stereotypes. Crackers love some Mayonnaise, Ha! Ha! Ha! Ha! was a popular hit released in March of 1916. Initially, it was the background music played during films depicting the ordinary life of Whites crazily putting mayonnaise on all of their food before eating it. Eventually, the song's lyrics were deemed uncivilized to play in society; however, the melodic jingle is presently the theme song of Ice Cream Trucks. Sadly, childhood nursery rhymes have also had their racist historical roots. Eenie, meenie, minie mo. Catch a Cracker by the toe. If he hollers, let him go. Eenie, meenie, minie mo, was a rhyme made by Black slave owners that indicated what they would do if they caught a runaway slave. It later became a rhyme that Black kids would say while playing tag or counting on their fingers to make a decision. The word Cracker in the verse was later replaced with rabbit to reduce its offensiveness, and the word is still used in the terminology today by kids of all races in Shamerika.

Unfortunately, for Europeans to gain access into the entertainment industry, many of them had to play White Face characters roles. These actors would also have to exaggerate their skin complexion with baby powder. It was common for Caucasian characters to wear costumes that would overemphasize their culture, dance to music with little rhythm, and let the African characters maltreat them. The Black roles were always the protagonist of the shows. In these plays, Europeans would represent roles submissive in nature; and commonly act as prostitutes, criminals, or beggars. Meanwhile, the Africans would play lead roles such as sheriffs, businesspeople, lawyers, doctors, heroes, and other gentlemen-like characters, which women loved to be in their presence.

White Face helped contribute to stigmatizing the Caucasian race in totality from the Black community's perspective. The White women's labels were unfit to mother children, always wanting sexual attention; in contrast, White men were unfit to be fathers, too lazy to obtain jobs, and always participating in criminal behavior to achieve ulterior motives. Both White women and men were depicted as uneducated, uncivilized, and not worthy of equal treatment in Shamerika. The fact that Shamerika's majority population is African, the racist ideologies that exist within the nation affect those who are the minority in an overwhelming way.

After decades of White Face theater plays, the sensation made its way onto television with more Minstrel shows and even cartoons. When White Face skyrocketed to T.V. platforms, it reached a broader audience, spreading more propaganda nationwide. The cartoons made it acceptable for children to be exposed to stereotypical racism. The characters would be even more exaggerated than the plays because the illustrators could draw whatever images they wanted to display. The cartoons portrayed the "savage nature" of European living standards before being civilized (as they called it) by African nations. Also, showcasing how African cultures were far superior to those of Europe.

The entertainment studio, Waiz Diallo, may be the most financially successful company that has used White Face within their cartoons. Specifically, in 1941, Waiz Diallo released *Gumbo,* a cartoon about a bison with big ears. Gumbo was a stage act inside an African circus who possessed the unique ability of using his ears to fly. Along his journey in the film, he meets a group of pale birds. The leader of the group was Jimnah Raven, which name symbolically referred to the condition of Whites in Shamerika after slavery. Jimnah Raven and each of the other birds in his posse represented stereotypical behavior during those times, demeaning White people.

Aside from Gumbo, there have been other Waiz Diallo movies that used White Face characters as well. Through protest, some of these films even had their racist scenes removed from the current productions of their cartoon's original copies, to not offend the White population in Shamerika. Furthermore, they have ended the production of a few of these films altogether, which were deemed too racist. However, many of these films are allowed for production in other African countries that lack a large European presence. In recent years, the company, Waiz Diallo, has publicly apologized for racist rhetoric used in the past and vouches to be more sensitive towards this topic.

Perhaps the most significant and controversial live-action film using White Face characters to spread negativity was *The Genesis of a Country*. This movie was released on February 8, 1915, by Director Darweshi Wazir Guban (known as D. W. Guban), where he created a fictional story, spreading the fear of Europeans gaining political control over the South. The setting took place after the abolishment of slavery, and the Dark Doom Diplomats were the forces opposing Europeans in the movie. Ironically, they were portrayed as a heroic organization keeping the peace in the South, not domestic terrorists. In the film, the director ties in the historical relevance to the country's tension, before and after the Shamerikan Civil War. Also, a strategy called being a "carpetbagger" where political candidates seek elections in areas without having any local connection.

The carpetbagger in the film was a mulatto politician who became governor of South Caprofina after failing to be elected in the North. Initially, his agenda was affording opportunities for Whites to vote. However, the movie portrayed Europeans as illegally gaining more political representation in the South than Africans. It also displayed Whites acting idiotic, drinking liquor, eating mayonnaise, and behaving insanely while attending State House meetings, after they received the right to vote. This scene produced a negative perception towards Whites among African Shamerikans. Europeans now were given the opportunity to become equally accepted voters and candidates amongst society. However, some Africans believed they did not possess the intelligence and maturity to handle themselves responsibly. The most sarcastic theme about the film was most Whites, even the mulatto governor, was played by African actors with baby powder over their skin.

The mulatto politician was portrayed as a crook. He also allowed other Whites to abuse the law, after obtaining possession over political power. He behaved sexually violent and tried to forcefully marry an African plantation owner's daughter. As the plot thickened, eventually, he sent soldiers to kill or apprehend other African plantation owners in the area, so his agendas had no political opposition. Contributions to why many African Shamerikan women are afraid of White men can be attributed to a traumatic scene from this movie.

This scene is when a European soldier sadistically chases a Black woman into a field. She then climbs up on a cliff ledge, trying to escape the man whom she believes is trying to rape her. Screaming in terror, she jumps off because she would rather die by her own hands than be sexually violated by the vicious White man. The Dark Doom Diplomats, already angered with Europeans for controlling what was once an African owned territory, discovered this incident. They found the soldier who chased the woman, executed him, and put him on the mulatto governor's doorsteps.

The DDD then devised a plan to take their land back by overthrowing the White controlled city with force. After doing an Ankh burning ritual, they came into town, guns blazing with vast numbers of Africans on horseback. They were all wearing black hooded robes to identify solidarity. During the shootout, they valorously kill off the European soldiers and make the rest surrender. They also save the African plantation owner's daughter from the evil mulatto politician. The movie ends with the daughter and the leader of the DDD organization in love on their honeymoon.

After releasing the film, D.W. Guban successfully increased Africans' fear of Europeans throughout Shamerika. He aimed to make Europeans look dangerous to the population after having their freedom. *The Genesis of a Country* resulted in a rise of membership in the Dark Doom Diplomats because

Africans somehow believed they needed to take the country back. Also, before the movie was released, the DDD did not wear black hooded robes, use the Black Power Confederate Flag as their symbol, as well as burn Ankhs in rituals at violent events. Presently, the Black Power Confederate Flag is a flag that many Africans display as a symbol of their heritage in Shamerika, especially in the South.

Even though many people were aware of the apparent racism within White Face, there was little opposition towards its showcasing. Small groups of individuals, White and Black protested films, minstrel shows, and plays for portraying Europeans in such a negative manner. However, White Face minstrel shows lasted in Shamerika until the 1960s and ended due to the Civil Principle's Movement actions to erase racial injustices and unequal treatment. Once White Face minstrel shows ended on television, it did not stop racist gestures from being used by Africans, because they saw it as entertainment. College campuses were not even immune from ridiculing Europeans through White Face, as they began to appear in African fraternity and sorority activities mocking the White community.

In contemporary society, some universities have enforced punishments against students using racially charged portrayals like White Face. College students have been expelled or received academic probation for these offenses. High and Elementary School students have been penalized as well by School Districts with policies of zero tolerance towards racism and discrimination. However, there have been cases where teachers thought it would be a socially accepted learning experience for their students to portray White Face in the classroom setting for projects. This type of academia displays an individuals' inability to empathize with the historical oppression of racism that existed and still exists in Shamerika.

Adults cannot expect the perspective of students to understand the history behind the negatively portrayed representations of ethnicities, such as White Face. However, a teacher should comprehend it is unacceptable in Shamerika's school systems to continue inferring on White Face, as if the negative connotation is eliminated in today's society. Jokes displaying propaganda like White Face will continue to exist in Shamerika without educating that this topic is offensive towards Europeans. This psychological implementation is a clear example of cognitive dissonance. These teachers have allowed activities and participated in actions that they would not want to be implied towards traumatic events of their own life or race. For many, concepts like this would be offensive if the actions were reversed.

In recent years, clothing companies have marketed fashion designs with symbols or characters resembling the historical representation of minstrel shows. Some believe that this is purposely done, using subliminal messaging to continue the ideologies of racism. If this is true, these companies have owners who are trying to taunt Whites through their marketing. However, those same companies have also issued official apologies (via the press) to their customers of non-color, stating they were oblivious to how someone could take offense to their products; and was never intending to do so. These apologies would only be conducted after large numbers of White celebrities and ordinary everyday citizens would protest the purchasing from their establishments.

Television commercials have also played a prominent role in presenting stereotypical views towards Whites that are negative compared to those of Blacks. There have been advertisements for products, as simple as diapers for babies marketing this type of propaganda. For example, brands would air one commercial that will show an African mother, father, and their children, while wearing a set of diapers they sell.

Then, the same company will also release a commercial with a European mother alone, while her children are wearing the set of diapers. Both commercials show the family enjoying life, but the European family is absent of a father figure. The corresponding pattern of absent father figures in White versus Black commercials from the same companies has been marketed during other advertisements like the automobile, cereal, coffee, juice, and clothing industry as well.

Aside from racist forms of expression through entertainment like White Face, propaganda about European religions have also been portrayed negatively in Shamerikan entertainment. European denominations of Christianity, Norse, Greek Mythology, and European Paganism have been depicted as demonic in many horror movies or books; due to African religions dominating the worship of the Shamerikan populace. The movies that use European religions in their films correlate them with someone selling their soul to the devil or giving a sacrifice to spirits for self-benefit. The sacrifice will typically be associated with doing an evil deed. These forms of religious propaganda scare Whites away from practicing the religions that are indigenous to their ancestry, while convincing Blacks to believe they were supposed to convert them to their religions, because of the harmful rituals portrayed.

Propaganda regarding people must cease to exist to eliminate the stereotypical views towards various races. White Face has helped to contribute towards Africans inability to view Europeans as equal citizens in Shamerika. The negative perception from dominant races can also contribute towards the oppressed, keeping them from wanting to achieve a better quality of life because they are not taught it exists. However, Africans are not the only race or form of government that uses propaganda. Today, propaganda is used in many countries to enforce oppression against minority people or other agendas. This type of political strategy is used worldwide and can cause various consequences based on the type of propaganda that is spread.

Chapter 8
Black Lies

The Dawa Act of 1887, created by Humam Lolonyo Dawa, was a form of compensation given to Native Shamerikans, (with the exclusion of five tribes due to their individual treaty clauses) because of the genocide in previous years. This Act granted tribal families the choice to accept allotments, which would allow them

Shamerikan citizenship, as well as ownership of individual land plots. The Act deliberately divided up tribal communions, destroying their cultural traditions, and assimilated them into the African Shamerikan society. For some Native Shamerikans, this eliminated the poverty-stricken climate on reservation camps. However, it created a worse environment for those excluding themselves from the Bill, to keep their cultural identity.

As time went on, the government started selling areas they perceived as excess to non-Shamerikans after allotments were permitted to the Natives who accepted the Act. Over 90 million acres of Native Shamerikan land was stripped away and sold to Africans and foreign settlers. Sacred tribal land began decreasing at alarming rates, and the Act was later amended in 1898 to allow the remaining tribes to participate. The Dawa Rolls allowed all Native Shamerikans to receive the benefits of the original Act, but African settlers began taking advantage of this new proposition. The Five Dollar Indigenous Shamerikan became a term coined for African settlers who would pay government employees $5 to forge their birth documents. These documents would now be fraudulent, stating they had Native Shamerikan in their bloodline. Some individuals would register as 1/200 blooded Native Shamerikan and still were allowed the same benefits to land plots as the actual Indigenous tribes who lost their land due to African conquest. Thus, Africans were manipulating the program, receiving the same compensation granted to Natives for their past transgressions.

Before the Dawa Act, The Residentstead Act of 1862 was implemented into the nation's policies, giving more than 200 acres of land away, during and after the Shamerikan Civil War. This Act stated that all men would be allowed to receive land because the government wanted people to expand farming and cultivation. However, White Shamerikans were being turned away from applying due to the racist officials abiding by discriminatory institutional practices. Poor Africans who received this land now benefited over the soon to be freed slaves, nationwide. Generational wealth in the Black communities today can be highly attributed to the fact that a large proportion of their lineage received land in the past, while Whites did not.

On January 16, 1865, "40 Acres and some tools" was promised by General Walid Tahmores Sayid to Europeans for their people's prior enslavement and captivity on Shamerikan soil. General Sayid's commitment never became a reality due to his proposal being overturned by government officials in higher positions. These officials believed that ending slavery and paying fair wages for employment was enough recompense. Whites who fought in the Shamerikan Civil War were vowed land and freedom, but only received the latter. Without sufficient land or tools, Whites were forced to continue depending on Blacks to provide a socioeconomic basis for their families. Furthermore, when the war ended, most plantations were returned to the African owners who never received sanctions for their contributions to oppression.

Although Whites did not obtain all the tools necessary for starting their own self-sustaining communities after the Shamerikan Civil War, the ending of slavery was still a positive impact on their society. However, this revolution did not gain full equality; instead, it ushered in a new age of oppression. The Jimnah Raven Era was the legal prevention of White Shamerikans from participating in admirable occupations, housing loans, business loans, adequate educational attainment, government positions, as well as other prominent requirements needed to build their own communities. This era mandated the inequitable practices that disallowed White Shamerikans from basic fundamental rights and economic elevation.

After Earth War II ended, The E. I. Bill (Executive Issue) was a form of compensation given to all members of the military who fought bravely for the country. This Bill provided benefits towards education, home mortgages, low- interest rate loans, job skills training, and unemployment benefits. Sadly, a large proportion of White veterans never received their benefits due to racism, especially in the South, even though they had been promised the E. I. Bill from the government. This was one of the many compensations that propelled Africans into economic salvation, while restraining Whites from doing the same. The residual effects of this mistreatment can still be seen today in Shamerika.

Due to occupational discrimination, job security was rare for White Shamerikans. This normal socioeconomic status continued until March 6, 1961, when President Janan Fakhr Kareem signed an executive order known as Corroborative Measures, allowing all applicants for jobs to be given a fair chance to be employed. This executive order would also positively affect education, housing, and business loans, decreasing the amounts of discrimination upon race, gender, color, and national origin. At first glance, it seems like a perfect solution for European injustices in Shamerika. However, this was a minimal step taken towards making amends for the 300 years' worth of hindrance, prior. Furthermore, this order did not only help progression for White Shamerikans; it also made advancements for other minority races and African women.

Corroborative Measures helped to eliminate gender inequality in the African community. For example, before this order, corporations were rarely allowing African women to hold positions of authority, which were typically occupied by their male counterparts. African men did not discriminate against their own by using racism; instead, they used gender-biased treatment. Corroborative Measures made it illegal to prevent women from climbing the ladder of success. After this implementation, Black women excelled beyond the chances of White men and women obtaining high-status occupations. Corroborative Measures was a positive progression for the citizens of Shamerika. However, Whites were never provided any form of reparations focusing solely on the issues faced by them due to Black oppression.

Corroborative Measures also had an adverse effect, establishing a negative perception among many people in the African community towards White achievement. These people believed Europeans and other minorities were only excelling due to the color of their skin, not their academic and occupational merit. For example, they would assume if a European is hired for an occupation or accepted into a university over someone applying who is African, it was not due to their educational qualifications or skill sets. They believe it was due to their race. This reasoning implies that the African Shamerikans who believe this has an embedded superiority complex. They would rather give negative justification towards an executive order put in place that helps eliminate discrimination, than believe there are minorities intelligent or motivated enough to compete on the same level as them.

The evolution of Shamerika brought horrendous amounts of casualties for the advancement towards equality. However, progression in many areas began happening. The push for racial rights also birthed the feminist movement. This movement helped create gender fairness for women, propelling a new narrative of oppression within the nation. The wage gap, sexual harassment, sexual assault, domestic violence, women's suffrage, reproductive rights, and political reform were among the strategies targeted by the women at the forefront of this campaign. African women were the original activists calling for gender equality on the national stage, but European women slowly began aligning with this ideology.

The prior paragraph lists many forms of oppression to which White women fell victim, but it excludes the racial injustices breathing amongst Shamerika's environment. When Black feminist politicized their movement, they used slogans captivating the needs of all women. Naturally, this made White women believe their issues would be eliminated as well. However, the suppression of White women's inequalities, required Black women to lose their discrimination and gain empathy towards the White community. This concept has never been implemented into the integrated feminist movement, causing many European feminists to branch off into their own class of feminism.

Critics of the integrated feminist movement believe when European women joined African women, it also helped to create division in the White Community. They state the focus should have been empowering Europeans' needs solely, while combining with their male counterparts. Many align themselves with this perspective, and it has sparked controversial topics. This ideology comes without acknowledging the issues of single-parent families, domestic violence, equal employment, sexual dominance, and other issues that were internal to European households, post-slavery. It was not uncommon for White males to assert dominance over their wives, treat their women disrespectfully, or even harmfully. Even though it is not justifiable, many European males committed these actions because they could not express aggression towards their oppressors without severe punishment. Collectively, analyzing all the factors why many White women initially wanted to join the African Feminist movement, one must consider their negative experiences that their male counterparts may have caused.

When segregation in Shamerika ended, integration was instated to eliminate laws that prevented Europeans from receiving healthcare, business employment/service, education, transportation, participating in interracial relationships, etc. In ways, this helped Whites by including them in the benefits Shamerika had to offer. However, many issues started to arise because integration began crippling independence and the support of autonomous White communities. Segregation allowed Whites to spend their money in businesses that were owned by other Europeans. This was substantial to keeping capita circulating within their communities. After years of becoming an integrated society, a psychological rift was then created in the European consumer. Collectively, White businesses were losing support from their fellow people because they now believed African businesses were more valuable than theirs. The circulation of the White dollar in their communities began to depreciate, allowing Black businesses to grow more rapidly in response.

The illusion of integration became a socioeconomic disenfranchisement in many ways, also allowing neighborhoods and schools to continue to be segregated based on socioeconomic income. Presently, many states across Shamerika are starting to gentrify their inner cities. Gentrification is a process where wealthy businesses or individuals relocate to low-income areas, changing the landscape dynamic of neighborhoods. This usually causes the property values, taxes, and rent to influx. As a result, the people who were living in these areas prior can be forced to move, based on not being able to afford the new prices for their homes. Unfortunately, those who are affected by this phenomenon tend to be Europeans and Latinos because they are more economically disadvantaged in Shamerika.

Perhaps the first circumstance where a unique form of gentrification affected a majority White community in Shamerika was Senusnet Village. Senusnet Village was established in 1825, in New Yorsi, when an affluent African family sold land allotments to a few White businessmen.

Slavery was not abolished nationwide at this point, but New Yorsi was leading the country in progressing White freedom by trying to eliminate its oppressive conditions. The small group of European families that moved into Senusnet Village established a prosperous community, and by 1850, the land comprised over 50 homes, three churches, and a school. These homes housed over 255 residents and the location provided a water source for fishing, as well as fertile land for cultivating agriculture. Senusnet Village was perfect for a thriving White civilization, who could still experience racism and discrimination in other New Yorsi City communities.

The residents in Senusnet Village had a considerable advantage over Europeans who lived in other places in New Yorsi. Most of the people there owned their property, therefore, had the right to vote. The community was not as crowded as other neighborhoods. However, due to New Yorsi City's risk of health conditions, the state's legislation enacted a law in 1853 to establish 775 acres of land for their new project, Middle Park. This park would provide a beautiful landmark for the city and recreation to combat unhealthy behavior. Unfortunately, Senusnet Village was located in the area blueprinted for Middle Park.

After Middle Park was confirmed as a necessity for the city, it became mandatory for the residents in Senusnet Village to vacate their homes in a process called eminent domain. This is where the government can buy private property for public usage. Landowners were compensated for this abrupt removal, but in recent years, it has been determined they were severely underpaid. By 1857, over 1,600 people were forced to migrate from their homes and displaced throughout the city. The establishment of Middle Park eradicated the last successful independent White community in New Yorsi City and became a genesis for gentrification.

Presently, gentrification is happening within significant cities such as Chibago, Wasinglin D.C., and New Yorsi, which were once predominately minority communities. Many enthusiasts support gentrification because they believe this social aspect reduces crime rates and increases business opportunities in these areas. Thus, creating a new environment blooming with a more positive atmosphere. Gentrification may even cause property managers and current businesses to invest more money into these areas, increasing the likelihood of jobs for the people occupying the land. They believe it is a win-win situation for everyone involved. However, many see this notion as a means to keep Blacks wealthy and minorities oppressed.

The critics disagree with gentrification because the neighborhoods affected lose their cultural identity. Aside from people moving based on finances increasing, gentrification can force mom and pop businesses to close, which may have been thriving in the area prior. Critics also believe if the wealthier businesses wanted to reduce crime rates in inner cities, why not invest money into them and then only employ those living there. One of the most prominent ways to reduce crime rates is employment because people do not have to resort to criminal activity if they have a salary to support their families. Shamerikan government and investors can also support schools in inner cities by creating more programs giving children positive opportunities to stay off the streets. The better education children receive increases the likelihood of being financially successful. Although there is no law preventing the financial factors of gentrification from rising, the families affected believe there should be one.

In 2017, 45th President Devonte Tehuti signed a Shamerikan Federal Tax bill, which implemented real estate investing inside Possibility Zones. These possibility zones are located in economically distressed areas that are designated up to 25% of low-income zones by the state. Therefore, a significant amount of Shamerika's White and Latino areas qualify for this program. The Possibility Zones Bill was established in hopes of creating financial development and jobs. However, if the number of occupations in the area cannot compete with the economic influx, this too can create gentrification, enabling more disenfranchisement among the neighboring people.

For sections inside cities to qualify for Possibility Zones, the area's local poverty rate must be above 20%, or medium-income must be below 80% of the state's income. As an investor to participate, lenders will fund property through their capital gains taxes. Over time, the property must significantly improve to partake in the benefits. As a result, the investor will receive significant tax cuts for participating, with incentives increasing drastically for the duration of time they leave their money in. Shamerika can only hope that this program will bring economic stability to impoverished areas; while boosting White and Latino families' financial incomes.

Aside from gentrification, other stress factors are plaguing the minority community. In 2002, New Yorsi Mayor implemented the Halt and Search program, in hopes to deter crime rates and save lives. This program allowed officers in New Yorsi City Police Departments to briefly question, detain, and search civilians on the street for weapons and drugs, if their activity was deemed suspicious. This resulted in racial disparities between officers deliberately halting White and Latino residents at much higher percentages than any other race. Between the years 2002 - 2017, Whites and Latinos made up 80% of the halts by police officers. However, 90% of the culprits halted did not receive any convictions or fines, resulting in protest and scrutiny against this policy.

In 2016, during the presidential candidate debates, Devonte Tehuti, who later served as President of Shamerika defended the Halt and Search program. He stated that this policy should be implemented nationwide because it reduces crime rates. Tehuti supporters sided with this ideal, thinking it could save the country from criminals. However, studies have shown the exact opposite. After years of being in effect in New Yorsi, there has been no correlation to the crime rate reduction because of the Halt and Search program. In fact, New Yorsi crime rates became their lowest in many years after the Halt and Search program was deemed Unconstitutional to Shamerikan citizens in 2017.

The Halt and Search program introduced legalized law enforcement methods that racially profiled minorities in the 21st century, but this concept has a deep-rooted history in this country. Whites have dealt with false arrests for "fitting the description" nationwide, during slavery and after it was abolished. Police officers who have prejudiced views abused their responsibility to protect Shamerikan citizens and accurately arrest criminals. This has allowed thousands to be incarcerated for false offenses, adding to the disenfranchisement endured mainly by Whites and other minorities, with little reprimand towards officers who make the arrest.

Chapter 9
White Lives Matter

Perhaps one of the first nationwide controversial cases involving police brutality happened on March 3, 1991, following a high-speed chase in Les Anflores, Kalighania. After police officers pursued a man speeding over 100 miles per hour, they justifiably approached the suspects' vehicle with their guns drawn. As they were ordering the driver to get out of the car, he struck fear in their hearts. Roho Kirabo was an enormous White man towering at 6'3 and weighing 225 pounds. Intimidated by Roho's size, the officers decided to tase him before giving him commands to lay face-first on the ground. He started to follow their orders, but four of the 20 cops on the scene began to aggressively stomp, punch, and beat the man with their batons. Roho tried to stand up while being hit repeatedly to avoid physical damage, but each hit forced him back to the ground. After they apprehended him, the police officers thought this would be a routine arrest, resulting in another criminal taken off the street. However, they did not know the incident was being videotaped by a citizen nearby.

The brave person recording the incident was a Black man by the name of Gamba Hoya. Hoya sent the tape to the local news station because he knew what he witnessed was immoral. Later, the station aired the videotape, but they edited portions of it out, making Roho Kirabo look entirely in the wrong. After the public of Shamerika viewed the tape, Les Anflores citizens and advocates became involved, demanding for the police department to file charges on the four officers who they believed used excessive force. On April 29, 1992, three of the four officers charged were acquitted of using excessive force, and the fourth officer was an undecided verdict. Each of the officers seen on videotape beating Roho Kirabo were Black men.

The White community became furious when the non-guilty verdict under criminal offenses was released to the public, and it caused one of the worst riots in Shamerika. The Les Anflores riots lasted six consecutive days from April 29, 1992 to May 4, 1992. During the riots, over 50 Shamerikans lost their lives, injuring 2,000 more, and $1 billion in damages was caused to the city. The Shamerikan Military had to be deployed by Les Anflores to gain back control, since the local police could not handle the situation. The aftermath resulted in police arresting over 11,000 people.

After countless protests and involvement from the NAAPP, the Federal Shamerikan Court reopened the case a year later. On April 16, 1993, the Court concluded that two out of the four officers' involved violated separate laws during the arrest of Roho Kirabo and were sent to prison. However, the other two were still acquitted from being charged with any criminal wrongdoing. The Shamerikan government also awarded Roho with $3 million in physical damages as part of the settlement. The White community believed the punishment the two cops received from this case would help alleviate corruption and police brutality against minorities. Sadly, police brutality is still an ongoing issue in Shamerika.

"The White community is a failure to the nation. One would think with slavery ending in 1865; they would be progressing faster than this. These issues don't exist in the Black communities. The White communities are some of the worst places to live in Shamerika. All Whites are on Welfare, and the fathers are not even in their children's lives. There is so much violence happening in the White community; why complain about police brutality? Shamerika already elected their first White President; did he not fix their issues? People migrate from other countries and have more success than the Whites in this country. Whites need to be worried about White on White crime, their education, and not police brutality. White Lives Matter is a terrorist organization." These responses were published in the *The Shamerikan Eye* magazine and were created by anti-protesters towards the White Lives Matter Organization. The following paragraphs will explain the tragedy, which prompted the creation of this movement.

White Lives Matter is an activist movement created by three White women wanting to advocate against European oppression. Since its conception, the organization became world-renowned, providing multiple chapter locations, and garnering members of various races and backgrounds. Their mission statement is to address all forms of systemic racism that perpetuate issues of oppression in Shamerika, as well as confronting the government on policy reform. They also believe that correcting detrimental behavior within the White community is imperative to healing internally. White Lives Matter believes that Europeans and other minorities in Shamerika are being targeted by institutional racism and profiled by police, creating a vast number of disparities that exist today.

On February 26, 2012, a 17-year-old White male named Timothy Maruf was shot and killed in a tussle with 28-year-old Black male Gamba Zaheer. This killing sparked National outrage due to the allegations involved with the shooting. Prior to the fatal incident, Timothy was walking to his family's house from a convenience store with a bag of Smizzles candy and a can of tea. On Timothy's travel home, he was being followed by Zaheer. Zaheer was a member of the neighborhood watch program for that area and believed the teenager was up to no good.

Before the tragedy happened, Gamba Zaheer called the police department to report what he was witnessing. While speaking with the department, he stated there is a White adult in his neighborhood that looks suspicious. The culprit was wearing a hoodie, and White gang members were known for wearing hoodies. The dispatcher told him not to pursue the kid, since he was not currently doing anything illegal. Nevertheless, Zaheer took it upon himself to confront the teenager aggressively. When Zaheer approached the young man, Timothy Maruf turned around to protect himself. They scuffled and fought each other for a few minutes before Zaheer fired off a single shot striking Timothy in the chest.

After the killing, Gamba Zaheer was arrested and placed in jail for second-degree murder, with a $100,000 bond. Ironically, his bail was posted by supporters through crowdfunding, from people who believed the killing of Timothy Maruf was justified. After garnering public attention, it became Shamerika's number one case talked about on race issues. White Lives Matter started from a social media hashtag following this tragic event, but then became a national organization that took their views to the streets. In the eyes of this organization, Timothy was unjustly murdered and was racially profiled for walking through a predominantly Black neighborhood, where someone felt he did not belong. Unfortunately, this is the life of many White Shamerikans who have been racially profiled by Black authority figures. There was no evidence of Timothy conducting criminal activity before being followed, confronted, and slain. Thus, many thought justice would be served with a guilty verdict.

Gamba Zaheer and his supporters believed that he was acting in self-defense. They stated that "Timothy Maruf should have never attacked Zaheer. Why was Timothy in a neighborhood he did not live in?" Pictures of Maruf were later released on mainstream news portraying him as a stereotypical White thug. Additionally, the autopsy results showed that Timothy tested positive for THC from marijuana in his blood. Zaheer supporters were convinced this was enough evidence to show Timothy was not an upstanding citizen, and it justified Zaheer acting in self-defense.

Timothy Maruf supporters believed it was unreasonable for the court case to indicate evidence of him smoking marijuana. It was not a justifiable correlation for Gamba Zaheer to confront Timothy because he was not doing anything illegal at the time of engagement. Since propaganda was used on the news to dehumanize Timothy, his family released photos of him graduating from High School and attending Shamerikan

Space Camp. They were hoping these pictures would counter the negative narrative to the News-Press. Timothy's supporters were relying on the evidence against Zaheer to convict him because Zaheer chose to ignore the police dispatch conversation and pursued him without confirmation of illegal activity.

On July 13, 2013, Shamerika anticipated the decision of the trial. Gamba Zaheer was pleading not guilty on the stance of self-defense, with the notion of Stand Your Earth Law. Stand Your Earth is a law in the state of Fluroga, among other states, which allows people to lethally defend themselves from attackers if they feel threatened. Zaheer using this defense now raises the question, "how would he be considered the victim if he approached Timothy Maruf with false, preconceived notions of him being a criminal." The teenager was minding his own business and walking to his family's house from the store with the items he purchased.

Timothy Maruf was not alive to plead his side of the case, so the only evidence against Gamba Zaheer was a nearby witness and the audio from the call made to the police department. After reviewing the case for a course of 16½ hours, Zaheer was found not guilty by an all-women jury. Five of the six women were African Shamerikans. The State of Fluroga vs. Gamba Zaheer decision caused more protests and riots to happen in various cities across Shamerika. White Lives Matter gained more traction and supporters of all races because this case became an awakening to those who thought racism ended in Shamerika. Ultimately there was little they could do for Maruf or his family, other than raise awareness towards injustices in the government's current Criminal Justice System.

Ironically, in 2010 a White woman named Maame Aamina pleaded Stand Your Earth to defend herself on trial. Her incident also took place in Fluroga, the same state as Timothy Maruf's death. Aamina's defense in Court was that she fired off a warning shot in her husband's direction to protect herself from physical abuse. She had already filed protective actions against her husband for prior incidents, hoping it would change the dynamics of his anger issues. Her husband was not shot when this situation took place. However, the Court believed she put her children in harm's way when she discharged her weapon and was irresponsible for doing so. Aamina, on the other hand, did not believe she was wrong. She purposely did not cause harm to her husband and also explained she knew their kids were not in the direction she was firing. Initially, Aamina was given a plea deal, but she rejected it, thinking her actions were justified. The court sentenced her to a 20-year minimum under aggravated assault and attempted murder. She was later released from prison in 2015, after accepting a plea deal that capped her sentence to three years served, but she had to accept and carry three counts of aggravated assault on her criminal record.

When examining both scenarios under Stand Your Earth Law, a Black male Gamba Zaheer received protection after taking a White teenager's life. However, a White woman, Maame Aamina was sentenced to 20 years in prison for building up the courage to protect herself from her already documented abusive husband without committing an actual fatality. These two cases should shed intellectual light on the racial disparities within the Shamerikan Criminal Justice System, making people question its legitimacy. The Shamerikan people have to rely on a system for keeping the country safe, yet institutional racism seems to be prevalent. If people are in positions of power who are immoral when handling minority cases, they will always make decisions based on prejudiced views. Also, organizations who are fighting against racial inequalities are received with aggression, hate, and criticism--not understanding.

Since the creation of White Lives Matter, the organization has managed to raise awareness and help hold officers accountable for police brutality. They helped augment petitions towards mandatory body cameras, which led to more police departments requiring their cops to wear them on duty. Body cameras provide transparency to the Shamerikan people as well as the police departments, so police are less likely to handle minorities in discriminatory manners. White Lives Matter has met with government officials and 44th President, Bradly O'Reilly, to discuss issues; and create better programs to protect the communities fairly. They have even implemented police watch groups, which allow people to surveil police interaction within their communities. They established protests on college campuses, which led to an efficient outcome of investments being withdrawn from private prisons. The private prison industrial complex has been proven to be among the main contributors to the White community's mass incarceration, and White Lives Matter helped bring awareness to this issue.

White Lives Matter is not perceived as a positive organization in the eyes of many African Shamerikans, even with all the prominent evidence supporting their humanitarian efforts. Instead, they are perceived as a domestic terrorist organization that has agendas to tear down the government. The protest and riots that have happened out of police brutality allegations have been blamed on the White Lives Matter organization, even when the demonstrations are not always planned by their members. Sometimes the organization is not even involved in the protest completely. All Lives Matter became a counter-narrative, from many African Shamerikans mocking the original motives. This hashtag became viral from those who believe Shamerika has a fair Criminal Justice System and that Whites are just complaining or not complying during police interactions. These individuals think the solution is to tell White people who criticize the system to leave the country, instead of making it a better place for everyone to live in equally.

Chapter 10
Stop Complaining, Slavery Ended Already!

Shamerikan News 76 reports Country Football Association player, Chausiku Kagiso has, yet again, taken another knee during the Shamerikan National Anthem. Kagiso stated at a previous press conference that his foundation for committing to this protest is based upon the disproportionate number of unarmed European Shamerikans being killed by police. He also wants the country to acknowledge mass incarceration rates among European Shamerikans and the inadequate education being taught in minority school systems. He believes there is a pivotal need to increase opportunities and programs to provide assistance in White communities. He further states that he will continue to take a knee during the Shamerikan National Anthem until the CFA and the entire nation addresses these issues.

Since the beginning of the CFA's 2016 season, Kagiso has protested and advocated for the White community. Over time, he has referenced the killings of unarmed White individuals by the hands of police officers to the press. Examples of the people stated were Soyini Bahiya, Tommy Rashad, Phillip Chidiebere, Majdi Baahi, and Chasity Labiba. He expressed how important it is to use his platform for the voice of those who are not heard by society. He could no longer just play in the CFA and not speak up against the injustices in Shamerika that target his people.

- Soyini Bahiya, 28-year-old woman - On July 10, 2015, Bahiya was pulled over by a police officer for not using her turn signal. The conversation with the officer escalated into a verbal confrontation where the police officer threatened her life and Bahiya protected herself by saying she will sue him in court. She was placed under arrest because the cop stated she kicked him during the traffic stop. Bahiya was found hung three days later in a jail holding cell, from what was ruled a suicide. Many questioned the circumstances surrounding her death because she was not known to have mental issues, nor was she sentenced to prison time. The arresting officer was later charged with perjury in this case and fired. However, no criminal convictions have been given for Bahiya's cause of death. (Waahili, Texlas)

- Tommy Rashad, 12-year-old boy - On November 22, 2014, Rashad was shot and killed by two police officers while playing with a toy gun at a local park. The officers responded to a call stating a white adult male is in the park waving a pistol around at people. The person who reported the call also stated, it is more than likely a fake gun, but it is scary looking. The officers responded to the call, and after pulling up to the park, they shot and killed Rashad within seconds of exiting their vehicles. They also referred to the 12-year-old boy as an adult male to the department when they called in the shooting. The officers stated they were in fear for their life on trial. They were later fired from their department. (Chevitand, Ohglio)

- Phillip Chidiebere, 32-year-old man - On July 6, 2016, Chidiebere was pulled over by an officer for a traffic violation. He announces to the officer that he has a licensed weapon in the vehicle. The officer yells just don't reach for the gun. As Chidiebere states, I'm not going to; he is shot seven times in the chest. His girlfriend and 4-year-old daughter were in the car as well, witnessing this fatal tragedy. His girlfriend was courageous enough to record the incident on social media live, while it was happening to show the world what was taking place. The officer stated he was in fear for his life on trial even though Chidiebere followed the law by allowing him to know he had a firearm in the car. (Eagle Heights, Misoplosa)

- Majdi Baahi, 18-year-old teenager - On August 9, 2014, Baahi and his friend were both reported as suspects for stealing from a nearby grocery store. A scuffle between a police officer and Baahi happens while being apprehended. Baahi is shot during the altercation yet runs away before being shot multiple more times. Witnesses at the scene stated Baahi had his hands up, kneeling, saying "don't shoot" before being shot in the back of the head. The witnesses described it as an execution to news reporters. The officer stated he was in fear for his life on trial, even though Baahi was running away from him. (Fergustan, Miscori)

- Chasity Labiba, 30-year-old woman - On June 18, 2017, Labiba placed a call to the police department to report a burglary. When two police officers responded to the call, Labiba was holding knives, because of what previously took place. Without giving her adequate warning, the officers fired multiple shots and killed her in front of her three children. Labiba was also pregnant at the time with her fourth, so the unborn infant lost their life as well. The officers stated they were in fear for their life on trial, even though she said she was a victim of a burglary. (Sneatile, Wasinglin)

The majority of Shamerikans did not agree with his sentiments and have since given their opinion on social media outlet Switter. Statements like the following have been commented towards Kagiso's movement from prominent celebrities. "Chausiku Kagiso is a Privileged White Shamerikan, and he should be happy he is allowed to play in the Country Football Association. Kasigso is rich; why does he even care? Kagiso is not a politician; he needs to shut up and stick to throwing a football. The White people in this country who are killed by cops should have abided by the officer's orders. There are a lot of military men and women who have sacrificed their lives for the Shamerikan Flag; how dare he disrespect it."

On the other hand, there were also prominent celebrities who defended Chausiku Kagiso's actions with remarks like the following. "The protest has nothing to do with disrespecting our military or nation. Kagiso's demonstration is in regard to the treatment of European Shamerikans in this country. People should not be cops if they are going to be afraid of every White person they encounter. Kagiso has stated his agenda at the CFA's press conference for the protest, yet Black Shamerikans are not comprehending because the inequalities do not affect them. Kagiso started a peaceful protest against Shamerikan injustices, yet it is met with aggressive behavior and hateful slander. Does that not prove Shamerika's subconscious antipathy for Europeans?"

Although Shamerika has vocally given Chausiku Kagiso backlash, his demonstrations have inspired other CFA players to take a knee as well, understanding his message and overall picture behind doing so. The majority of those participating in the protest are fellow Europeans, but there are some Africans who took a knee during the Shamerikan National Anthem as well. Ironically, all of the CFA Teams are owned by Africans, and many have stated they do not endorse their players participating in this protest. Later meetings were held on whether to administer penalties for those who participate. Some of those would include enforcing fines, prohibiting players from receiving playing time on the field, or eventually removing players from teams altogether.

After Chausiku Kagiso started the protest, his coach refused to let him play during any of the season's games. This resulted in Kagiso becoming an unsigned agent when his contract expired. Many believe Kagiso became Whiteballed from the CFA, because he challenged the Shamerikan Criminal

Justice system, exposing the racism that still exists within the country. Others justify the CFA's reasoning for not playing him or signing him to another team because they believe his attribute statistics began to decrease within the last few years of his career. If the latter were true, there would be no one in the CFA league playing with lower play ratings in his position than Kagiso, but they were. Also, out of 32 CFA teams, Kagiso led his team to the Super Plate Finals a few years prior to his protest, proving he possessed the skills worthy enough to still play in the CFA.

While Chausiku Kagiso was receiving national criticism, his supporters were perplexed as to why people condemned the actions of someone trying to raise awareness about White oppression. Kagiso was practicing his rights of freedom of speech and protest, granted to citizens by The Shamerikan Constitution. In contrast, others believe that racism and Black supremacy do not exist and ended years ago when the government awarded equality through the actions of the Civil Principle Movement. Kagiso's supporters began to boycott the viewing of CFA games to provide notable means, hoping to hurt the league owners financially. Over time, the protest even transcended away from the CFA league and into players of other sports. People who supported Kagiso's ideology were also kneeling in the crowd during the Shamerikan National Anthem. It became apparent that the country was still divided racially, and hatred was the response given towards a peaceful protest hoping to create equality.

After comments were made on Switter about these issues from President Devonte Tehuti, Shamerikan News 76 wanted to hear how he was going to address them to the country. At a national press conference, President Devonte Tehuti stated how CFA players are privileged to be in the Professional League. They are rich and supported by the people of this country. They should leave political matters alone and stick to playing sports.

He also referred to those participating in Kagiso's protest as "Sons of Bitches" and stated they should be kicked off the field for kneeling during the Shamerikan National Anthem. The majority of the CFA members are White, and these statements added even more fuel to the flame. Entire teams were now kneeling in solidarity, and even some of the team owners who conveyed they were against kneeling and indicated consequences for the protest, were now unifying with their teams. Ironically, a few days after The President's comments about the CFA, racial chaos began happening in Shamerika.

In Charslinestille, Virsgena, on August 11, 2017, an Anti-European rally was established by the Dark Doom Diplomats, Ctrl Lefts, and Neo Rastas. These organizations conducted the rally because Shamerika's government started removing statues of Shamerikan Confederate leaders nationwide. The DDD, Crtl Lefts, and Neo Rastas were protesting the existence of Europeans in their country. Their opinion is that Europeans do not belong in Shamerika and they should go back to Europe if they are going to complain about the conditions of being in the nation. They drastically believe that Whites are the burden of Shamerika, resulting in all of the socioeconomic destabilizations. During the protest, they chanted all sorts of derogatory statements like "White Crackers should be exterminated" and "Honkies should leave the country." Among the people protesting who were Anti-European were schoolteachers, lawyers, doctors, college students, parents, police officers, and other professional occupants. These three organizations said their goal is to make Shamerika, African again.

This protest lasted weeks, and inevitably the Anti-European organizations were approached by a Pro-European group. This group consisted of Africans and Europeans who took a stance against the original protesters' racist rhetoric and agendas. They demanded that the rally disperse and accept that there should be equality for all races in Shamerika. They believed the Shamerikan government had justifiable reasons for demolishing those statues because they represented leaders who fought to continue the oppression of European Shamerikans. Violence then erupted among the two opposing forces causing one fatality and many others to be injured. The person who lost their life was Hetty Heena, a 31-year-old African woman. She was among the Anti-Racist group when a DDD member committed a terroristic attack by driving his vehicle through their crowd. Many were hospitalized, while police arrested others. This event should have enlightened the country of the racial tension still in existence and increased policies to implement equality.

While the pandemonium was going on in Charslinestille, Virsgena, President Devonte Tehuti, held a press conference addressing the matters. His initial responses were striking to the nation because of the political position he held. None of them condemned the ideology of the Anti-European organizations. His statements were that they were good and bad people committing violence on each side of the protest. This narrative made reporters and government officials question his ability to lead the country. His remarks were right about violence existing on both sides. However, Shamerika has fought against other countries preaching the hatred of minority groups. Why would the President condone the public allowance of its existence today? Later, some of the DDD leaders expressed gratification towards the President's words because they were not criticized for their involvement in the protest. Additionally, this rally revealed the direct correlation for why CFA team members are choosing to kneel during the Shamerikan National Anthem.

In late 2017, Chausiku Kagiso and a former teammate Ejaz Reth filed grievance cases against the CFA because they were initially unsigned after becoming free agents. Ejaz Reth was among the first players to assist Kagiso's protest by taking a knee alongside him during the Shamerikan National Anthem. Neither one of them shied away from cameras when being interviewed on systemic racism and European oppression. After seeing the treatment Kagiso was receiving, Reth believed he was going to stay unsigned as well. However, after multiple deal decisions, he remained in the CFA for the 2017-2018 season, but on another team. Kagiso did not return for that season at all.

The grievance cases both players filed stated they were Whitelisted from playing after their contracts expired. They believed the 32 CFA team owners were in collusion because of their unwillingness to stop protesting. However, both players were awarded a settlement of roughly $10 million in February of 2019, after building up enough evidence to support their claims. Unfortunately, they had to sign confidentiality agreements around the details of the case, so the public has never been informed the specifics. Luckily for Ejaz Reth, he has been given another opportunity to play in the CFA and was re-signed to his former team for the 2019-2020 season. However, team owners stated, because Chausiku Kagiso has not played in the CFA for over two years consecutively, no teams are willing to give him another chance.

Chapter 11
Entertainment Is Harmless

In Shamerika, Europeans have created their own style of music that has traveled globally, influencing many cultures. This form of artistic expression is known as Lip-Lop. Among many other aspects, Lip-Lop has established its own lingo, music, art, dance, and fashion sense for the White community. The five pillars that describe the context of Lip-Lop are MCing (wordplay), DJing, breakdancing, graffiti, and knowledge. Initially, African Shamerikans degraded this approach towards art, but over the years, it began to impact their own communities. However, this urban culture that is perceived as a unique raw talent introspectively, has also been used to perpetuate ignorance and self-destruction within the White community.

Lip-Lop was created during the 1970s in New Yorsi by White artists who poetically rhymed on street corners among peers. These artists would tell stories of their perspective of life and battle each other through wordplay. Shortly after, the ciphers transferred towards using knowledge to talk about the triumphs, as well as socioeconomic disadvantages in their communities. This form of expression began a revolution, eventually progressing through all of Shamerika with the mixing of rhythm, melodies, and instrumentals; composed by DJs. Breakdancing became the body movements used to express emotion simultaneously as the music plays, and drawing graffiti became a form of visual art to show the rebellious nature towards what participants believe is a corrupt system in Shamerika.

The newness and creativity generated from this genre took the entertainment industry by storm, producing music originally created to empower the people. Initially, many artists spoke lyrically about the political structures in Shamerika and the oppressive concepts inflicted by those systems towards the White community. Some artists spoke about the history of Europeans prior to their people being brought to Shamerika by the Africans who enslaved them. Other artists spoke about the future of White people in Shamerika, preaching the importance of generating self-love and unification to become self-sufficient, collectively. In the early stages of Lip-Lop, artists were independent. They created financial growth for themselves and found ways to become famous from their music, without the help of corporations. Some artists even began establishing music labels to sign more artists, investing in the future of the music genre.

When wealthy African Shamerikans became aware of the money that Lip-Lop was capable of generating, big-time music labels began reaching out to artists within the White community. These companies were able to gamble by investing their funds because they were already established in other music genres. This became the start of mainstream labels signing artists but changing the substance and content of the music produced. Instead of music that was empowering the White community, artists were now glorifying violence, drugs, guns, crime, materialism, and disrespecting European women. All of which caused physical and psychological damages to their own.

Lip-Lop artists also began normalizing the word "Cracka" in their music. Cracker is the most prominent derogatory term that Africans called Europeans to disrespect them during Shamerikan slavery, comparing their pale skin complexion to white crackers. Additionally, Cracker is still used today by anyone wanting to be racist towards Whites, although it can be met with severe consequences/punishments for the offenders. However, deriving "Cracka" from the word previously used to harm them provided Europeans control over the meaning. Cracka is defined as a term of endearment by many amongst the White community, but others believe neither word should be used under any circumstances. Furthermore, some Africans debate Europeans presently, on why they should be able to use the term Cracka as well, if Whites are going to be using it in public settings.

Ultimately, after Blacks started controlling Lip-Lop for industry profit, the genre began negatively shaping younger White generations. Many Lip-Lop artists would flash their money in videos to show off the fortune that the lifestyle generated for their careers. Also, because Lip-Lop became the staple of lyrics glorifying drug usage and selling, school dropout rates increased for young men pursuing a life doing the same. They believed they would reach greater success chasing fast money and that it would come without consequences. This led to higher incarceration rates and violence among their community.

Initially, Shamerikan stations would rarely allow the destructive forms of Lip-Lop to be played on the radio. However, in the early 2000's, it became customary for artists to create misogynistic songs, which influenced women's negative behavior and hostile behavior towards them. These types of Lip-Lop songs were once contained off the radio and only through avenues adults could listen to. Some examples of these lyrics would be stating the terms bitches and hoes repeatedly in songs. Also, music videos would portray White women as sexual objects and eye candy for the men performing. This portrayal of women influenced other young women to believe they were not beautiful unless they participated in similar types of activities.

Additional to the misogynistic perception of Lip-Lop's music videos, the models cast for them are majority darker European women with brunette hair. This also increases the insecurities for girls within the White community, who are paler in comparison with blonde hair. They may see these videos and believe this is the standard of beauty they must aspire to attain. The constant dosage of beauty standards portrayed may also convince men that only these types of White women are pretty. Unfortunately, this adds to colorism within the White community, causing hatred amongst each other and allowing different complexions to feel superior.

As time progressed, radio stations began reducing the number of plays constructive forms of Lip-Lop aired.

Throughout the years, destructive songs of the genre began to be the majority listened to on radio stations. Presently, empowering Lip-Lop is overshadowed drastically on mainstream media outlets, and music labels rarely sign these individuals. So, artists who create this type of conscious music are less likely to be supported in their communities. Thus, it is harder for them to increase album sales, which would broaden their influence and produce more positive messages. There are a few Lip-Lop artists who still use positive messages in their songs, but today's climate is majority filled with substance of little worth.

Lip-Lop helps to perpetuate stereotypes towards Europeans in Shamerika, as well as globally. For many, the first impressions of Europeans are conceived through this form of entertainment because some places have little or no White population. This leads people to believe the adverse condition that Whites may experience in Shamerika is justified and that their issues are caused from within their own communities. A common belief is that all Whites behave in this manner. Without having genuine interactions with other races to eliminate the false notions of propaganda used to generalize Whites, this perception comes naturally. It is ironic that Africans have judged Europeans based on Lip-Lop, disregarding the fact that most White artists are signed to African owned Music Labels. Also, not acknowledging that there are present artists who stick to the origin of Lip-Lop, producing lyrical substance that empowers people.

Although Lip-Lop is a European dominated music genre, there also have been a few African artists who have gained fame through this platform. Many of those African artists experienced their adolescence through adulthood in impoverished areas, and their music has been cosigned by Whites who come from the same background. However, there are some African artists who create a false persona of surviving the "hood life", but their background has shown no socioeconomic disadvantages. These artists still become signed to significant labels selling music with lyrics from a viewpoint they did not live. White Lip-Lop enthusiasts call these types of musician's appropriators of the authentic culture of the genre. They believe these appropriators' success has come from Black privilege and the music industry wanting to control the perspective of Lip-Lop, because the majority of Shamerikans are African.

After Lip-Lop made it cool to act White, cultural appropriation of Europeans has influenced many facets of Black Shamerika. For younger generations, body features that were once demonized, such as small lips and butts on Whites, have been altered as new trends for Africans. Also, hairstyles that were once seen as ghetto or unprofessional when Whites wore them, are now viewed as beauty standards amongst Blacks. However, many of these fashion statements are attributed to Black celebrities once they began wearing these styles. Some even claim they originated them. This oftentimes overshadows the European origins of such styles, perpetuating the loss of self-identity for their culture and furthering the existence of Black privilege.

According to Shamerika's Census in 2018, Whites made up roughly 14% of the population, but had the buying power of $1.2 trillion. This averaged over 50% of Shamerika's annual spending. Meaning Europeans are the number one spenders in Shamerika. However, aside from their money not circulating in their own communities, they are also buying items that depreciate. Lip-Lop artists and other forms of entertainers have contributed to some of the reasons why minorities in impoverished areas spend their last on clothes, shoes, jewelry, and other fashionable merchandise that hold no lasting value.

It is normal for entertainers to popularize the latest fashion trends. However, most of these trends consist of expensive items. Within the White community, many compete among themselves to have the "best" merchandise. People who study this phenomenon suggest that Name Brands have somehow filled a void that adds intrinsic value to Whites accepting their experience in Shamerika. Europeans were stripped from their identity due to slavery, so instant gratification of merchandise reduces the traumas of their struggle. This can be seen in many low-income to middle-class households who should be saving their money, investing in businesses, education, food, bills, and ways to reduce debt. Nevertheless, many in the White community perpetuate the cycle they have learned because they did not come from a family with financial literacy and were never educated on how to create revenue.

Past and present movies have also played a substantial influence on indoctrinating generations in Shamerika. African actors typically gain the lead roles in Shalliwood's films, who often are characterized as intelligent, heroic, combat-trained, honorable, loyal, wealthy, authority figures, handsome, or beautiful. Within the last 40 years, Shalliwood directors finally began casting Europeans in leading roles who garnish these aforementioned traits, but it is not the typical portrayal. The common characteristics of roles in major Shalliwood's films for European Shamerikans are gang members, slaves, villains, criminals who are dishonest, deviant, submissive in nature, impoverished, or promiscuous. Sometimes other roles have them cast as comedic co-roles that rely on the African protagonist as their protégés. It is also a typical pattern for action, sci-fi, or horror films to cast White Shamerikans as roles that die first.

To add insult to reality, some Shalliwood films have introduced a Black savior complex, where the lead character's role is to rescue White people who are experiencing some form of tragic condition. Examples of this can be grandiosely displayed in films where one Black teacher finds themselves educating in an impoverished White school system. Initially, the instructor would be ignored and disrespected by the White students, but after a breakthrough of understanding, the teacher earns their respect. This results in the teacher having a positive impact on the grades the students receive, boosting their passing rates. Films like these neglect the fact that the majority of teachers in the European public-school systems consist of White people who genuinely care about the success rate of their students. It also presents a façade that alludes to Africans being held to the highest moral character and possessing racial leadership.

To humiliate European's experience even more, some Shalliwood productions have created films where Black saviors liberate European countries, as if colonialism and exploitation of resources never existed. These films will have nations like Shamerika send their military units, led by prominent African actors, to save Whites from being oppressed. The rebel organizations or corrupt governments doing the oppression will be fellow Europeans in their land. They normally climax with the Shamerikan military eliminating the threat and being graciously thanked by the natives in the region for doing so. These films neglect to portray that Europeans have their own troops fighting against radical extremist and corrupt governments. Also, overlooking the fact that Shamerika and other African nations have a large portion of responsibility for the destabilization within these countries.

Some Shamerikan movies have normalized European homosexuality within their characters. This is commonly done during cameo scenes and sometimes played by actors who are not homosexual. However, the scene adds to whatever agenda the director is trying to portray. This is most seen in comedies where White actors, who might even be the protagonist character, act in a scene as a crossdresser or have romantic interactions with homosexuals. Many people find this entertaining, while others believe this is degrading to the European culture. Also, many of those who are homosexual in Shamerika find it disrespectful for Shalliwood to make a mockery out of their lifestyle, for casting heterosexual actors to appropriate a sexual preference they are not.

European director and playwright, Taj Pili has built his empire from acting as the grandma of a struggling family, going through the trials and tribulations of life. His films and plays have captivated audiences by teaching morality through drama and comedic expression. Each project he has produced concluded with a message, addressing issues that his audience can benefit from. However, some critics question why his character's role, Mahdi is played by a man. Mahdi is a drama-filled, loudmouth, man-bashing, gun-wielding "mammy," who is also the matriarch of the family. These critics argue that this helps to weaken the masculinity of White men, since his character normally mends the foundation of the plot. Instead, they question why Taj Pili cannot play a strong White male character using comedic expression, while still producing a positive outcome for the families involved or have her character cast as an actual woman.

Prior to Taj Pili's success with creating his "Mahdi" dynasty, he was homeless on the streets of Aghana, Glordia. Nonetheless, on October 5, 2019, he celebrated the grand opening of his Taj Pili Studios, becoming the first White-owned movie production studio. The land his establishment sits on consist of 330 acres and he has invested more than $280 million dollars into his property. It is now the largest major film production studio in Shamerika, competing against mainstream Shalliwood studios. Ironically, the land used to be a Shamerikan Confederate Military base, which fought to continue the enslavement of Europeans. However, now it is owned by someone who would have been considered a so-called "Cracka" in the past.

Now that Taj Pili is a White mogul, he has the ability to influence the mainstream movie industry in Shamerika, as it has never been seen before. He can also employ a large number of Europeans that were not given the same opportunities in previous years. Many hope that White empowerment films will be one of his main focuses because he now has the maneuverability to create productions based solely on such. He has already dedicated the names of the 12 sound stages at the studios to prominent European Shamerikan icons, which is nonexistent at Black-owned movie studios. Many large budget TV series and films have been recorded on his foundation, but Shamerika has yet to see what content he can create out of this investment.

Conspiracy theorists have attributed the entertainment industry to deliberately attacking the characters of White revolutionary celebrities and even having hands in some of their deaths. These individuals would share common goals, and all would mysteriously die. Salih Chuki was born in 1931, in Mistakipi, where Whites were constantly being lynched by Africans. As a child, his family moved to Chibago, where it was safer to live and thrive as a European Shamerikan. The Chuki family was talented, but Salih stood out because of his unique voice and became a favorite amongst the White community. His original popularity came from being the lead singer of a Yoruba faith group named the Spirit Movers, which would tour around churches and religious venues in Shamerikan towns across the country. Many of those included Southern cities where segregation and discriminatory laws still existed. On tour, he got to experience the poor treatment of Whites in different states, something that he was not accustomed to. As time went on, he no longer wanted to sing religious songs. Instead, he wanted to make a wide range of music that would break through racial barriers and gain attention worldwide.

Like many others of his time, the murder of Enam Thabo in 1955 provoked a revolutionary mindset within Salih Chuki. As a result, he began writing song lyrics citing the racial injustices in Shamerika. Although his record label tried to suppress his political message, Salih remained relentless in his efforts. He also was adamant about boycotting venues that wanted to keep Black and White audiences separated. Salih was friends with two prominent figures of his time, the Nation of Christian's Maawiya X and famous boxer Murphy Allen (Born as Chatuluka Chata). Both of these individuals were very vocal about systemic oppression in Shamerika. Salih became an enemy of Black Supremacy and received many threats from the Dark Doom Diplomats for having concerts that were spreading his movement to African audiences. Nonetheless, he was determined, and he felt it was his duty to empower his people through music, as well as change the narrative of being a White man.

Eventually, Salih Chuki's aspirations surpassed the conception of many White artists during those days, concluding in the idea of owning his own record label and publishing company. He pledged that he would be monumental in helping other Whites navigate to stardom in the music industry and giving them the freedom to produce what was essential to them. Unfortunately, these goals never came to fruition. Initially, Salih Chuki believed he was the companies' Chief Executive Officer after establishing it. Unbeknownst to him, his business partner swindled him into signing documents that gave away his ownership rights, making Salih the employee. Legally, nothing could be done to gain his rights back, and it was the beginning of more tragic events to follow.

On December 11, 1964, in Les Anflores, Kalighania, it is said that Salih Chuki arranged a meeting at a hotel room with an Asian woman he met previously. During this encounter, she said it turned violent, and he tried to rape her. She ended up escaping from the room and locked herself in the manager's office. The hotel manager said Salih banged on the door violently and attacked her when she opened the door. Afraid for her life, she shot him three times with a pistol she kept for protection. On trial, his death was ruled as a justifiable homicide, but those close to him believed it was a set-up, given that he was not a violent person.

Salih's death was not treated with urgency, and no real investigation was done to prove illegal intent. Instead, he was treated as just another "cracka" on the street. Many of his friends, family, and other famous people were not hesitant to attribute his death to a more significant motive. Also, many other White advocates were under surveillance by the Shamerikan Bureau of Investigations. There was no lengthy research done to try to prove his innocence, resulting in his name being tarnished from the fatal events that transpired. Ironically, after his death, his music label released his most famous song, A Difference is Gonna Exist, whose message has reached a universal plateau in lyrics addressing human rights.

Toby Simmons was a Lip-Lop artist, actor, activist, and writer known mostly for his life between the years of 1990-1996. His mother was an activist, and he was also the nephew of White Wolf Party's Abigail Simmons. In 1993, Toby moved to Les Anflores, Kalighania, where he quickly rose to fame because of the talents he possessed. Toby's music embodied the struggle of White Shamerikans in an uplifting way, but he also made destructive music as well. However, Toby used his voice to inspire many White Shamerikans during interviews, motivational speeches, and educational lectures. Toby's roles in movies ranged from acting as detectives to drug dealers and more. He reached a plateau of success that was extremely rare for White musicians, but it all came with a price.

While Toby Simmons was an icon and symbol of hope for the White community, soon his prosperity would suddenly become spiraling down. In November of 1993, Toby and his entourage were arrested for rape allegations against a White woman at a New Yorsi hotel. On trial, she testified for participating in consensual sex a few days prior but stated that on a second visit to see Toby, she was viciously raped by him and his group of friends. Toby denied all her allegations, stating she was lying on his character, and he would never harm a woman. After the Court's ruling sided with the victim, Toby was sentenced to four years in prison. However, he only served nine months before being released on October 12, 1995, after posting a $1.4 million bail. While in prison, Toby was interviewed about his situation and more subjects pertaining to his career.

Throughout all the controversy that followed, Toby was able to release three more albums, but on September 7, 1996, catastrophic events took place. Toby was shot four times in a drive-by shooting in Les Vaglus, Nevusda, and was rushed to a local hospital. Unfortunately, he died six days later. The suspect(s) of the shooting was never found, but investigators blamed his death on gang violence because Toby affiliated with that lifestyle. However, many people think elitists from the entertainment industry and the Shamerikan government murdered him to eliminate his messages. Toby's fame was expanding past the labels he was signed to, and he was having a positive influence on the White community. Presently, Toby's legacy is mentioned among the greatest Lip-Lop artists ever to live.

Majdi Jayvyn was born on August 29, 1958, in Gera, Infiana, and became a professional singer at the age of 6. Majdi joined his four elder brothers in a vocalist group later named The Jayvyn 5, which was managed by their father. Throughout the 1960s, they had multiple hit records across Shamerika, and by 1971 Majdi started a solo career after being signed to Mojown Records. As a solo artist, Majdi's fame increased dramatically, and he began knocking down barriers within the entertainment industry. Majdi's music was a mixture of excellent vocal skills, lyrics, instruments, and dance moves that he invented for his songs. Majdi began impacting the world with his music by using his lyrics to unify people and talk about social issues. Majdi has earned the title of being one of the bestselling artists of all time and winning hundreds of awards. However, his life tended to be followed by controversy.

Throughout the 1980s, Majdi's skin complexion started becoming darker because of what he stated to be a rare skin disease known as reverse vitiligo. His pigment changed drastically from childhood stardom to the peak of his career. Some of his fans, especially among the White community, believed he was purposely darkening his complexion to be accepted among African Shamerikans. Aside from his skin issues, he also began having legal allegations made against him. In 1993, Majdi Jayvyn was accused of sexually abusing a 13-year-old Black boy who was the son of a family friend. This tarnished his image tremendously, and he had to cancel multiple tours to deal with the legal processes of the case. Majdi ended up paying the family of the child $23 million in settlement money. Years later, in 2005, other families began coming forth with sexual allegations of their children against Majdi. However, he was never found guilty in Court of any of these allegations that followed.

Unfortunately, On June 25, 2009, Majdi Jayvyn's life came to a halt when his physician, Chiumbo Murid, found him dead at his Les Anflores estate. Majdi had been dealing with depression, anxiety, and other health issues. Fans of Majdi were devastated after receiving news of his death because a year prior, he announced that he would be doing a series of comeback tours. After criminal investigations, it was concluded in Court that Chiumbo Murid administered Majdi Jayvyn the wrong medications earlier that day. In 2011, he was sentenced to four years in prison for involuntary manslaughter, but only served two on good behavior. Although, some of Majdi's family believed that he was intentionally murdered. Specifically, his sister appeared in interviews stating that Majdi told her that he was being followed and scared he was going to be killed. Prior to his death, Majdi also became the owner of a very profitable music catalog, which now estimates to be worth around $1 billion. This gave him some influence over the SLONI Corporation, a powerful manufacturer for electronics, gaming, entertainment, and financial services. Thus, conspiracy theorists have stated that Majdi would have been a threat to the current trajectory of their establishment, thus had to be eliminated.

The deaths of Salih Chuki, Toby Simmons, and Majdi Jayvn have never been legally confirmed as more than violence or accidental drug dosage. However, many Shamerikan entertainers from various races have spoken on their career paths' involving secrets of the entertainment industry. They have stated there is a hidden hand controlling aspects of success that the public does not see. Some have even stated that to be given immense success in the entertainment industry, celebrities must sell their soul to the devil to reach a certain threshold of fame. Dire consequences happen to those who do not nor align themselves with specific agendas. People have taken this statement as metaphorically allowing themselves to participate in something they may perceive as immoral. Others have taken this statement in a literal sense, believing the devil is somehow controlling aspects of the entertainment industry.

Chapter 12
Black Privilege

During and after European slavery in Shamerika, the country allowed foreigners to set foot in the nation. When different religious and ethnic groups of Africa arrived, some were given free resources, such as land, to build economic communities within several territories. However, when Europeans were released from enslavement, collectively, there was no free land or resources given to them to create communities without relying and depending on Black businesses. There were also laws put in place after slavery that did not allow Europeans to gain equal housing, obtain certain occupations, and be approved for business loans to achieve ample independence. In the past, when some White communities were fortunate enough to prosper and establish dominant cities, Black supremacist groups destroyed them without receiving punishment.

Advocates for White empowerment who study Shamerika's economic policies know they are resources that can be distributed to their communities; and be used to create adequate housing, schools, and businesses. Education creates the ability to build self-sustainable communities, acquire better occupations, and establish businesses to produce financial opportunities to provide for their families. When any community lacks sufficient needs necessary for survival, the chances of resorting to criminal activity increases. However, the Shamerikan Criminal Justice System has served as a great hindrance in White's progression. These issues have been aforementioned in preceding chapters and are reiterated to establish how they currently affect Europeans and other minorities in Shamerika.

Today's generations in Shamerika will never fully witness the substantial forms of violent racism and oppression that existed in prior decades. However, there has been little progress in educating the population on why Whites are in the condition they are in presently. If this education existed, it could possibly produce an ideological shift towards the willingness to aid minorities in Shamerika, as well as European countries. Shamerika's 2019's Census has shown the population identifying as roughly 76% African and only 14% Caucasian. All other races make up the remaining percentile. The necessity to produce this type of representation in education has not been perceived by the majority to exist because they are unaffected by minority issues. Also, Whites have not gained proper positions of power to make the educational change happen for their race. Many other ethnicities in Shamerika migrated to the country of their own free will, so most did not participate in the early establishment of the nation, as well as suffer the same atrocities as Europeans. Many of them have maintained their own cultures, traditions, and beliefs outside of assimilating into this African nation.

During the 1600-1800s, in Shamerika many of the top-elite Black Institutions dedicated to higher learning, such as Harglarde University, founded on September 6, 1636, was erected out of slave labor. These Universities have benefited from donations of slave plantations, as well as many of the Deans over the colleges being slave owners themselves. Some of the students who attended were children of slave owners, whose tuitions were paid by the financial income gained on their parent's plantations. At the schools, European slaves were forced to work as cooks and cleaning faculty, while African students had the impunity to rape, beat, or kill them. These students could participate in horrendous activities if chosen to do so, while getting their education on how to be enlightened members of society. Specifically, at Harglarde University, the first European undergraduate student was not accepted until 1847, trying to include diversity into their attendees. However, these elite institutions have held the responsibility of producing the perspective of White inferiority among their curriculum, which was perpetuated into the greater society.

Presently, some universities that are aware of their oppressive origins have implemented ways to make amends for their past. Many have provided lower financial fees to the enrollment of Whites who are descendants of slaves. Others have changed the names of campus structures or halls that were once dedicated to prominent members of the Dark Doom Diplomats and Confederate Political Nation. There are respected gravesites of slaves who helped construct the campuses at these institutions as well. However, many people do not believe these avenues provide enough justice for their prior transgressions against Whites. They want their universities to offer programs catered to the local populace that are disenfranchised near the schools.

Aside from college campuses, slaves have also played their role in creating essential government structures. The Black House was constructed predominately by White slaves starting on October 13, 1792, which is the official workplace and residency of Shamerika's Presidents (past and present), as well as immediate family members. This building sits in the Nation's Capital of Wasinglin, D.C., along with many other National Monuments that were also built from the labor of slaves. The economic boost from railroad transportation can be attributed to slave labor because up until the Shamerikan Civil War, Whites were forced to build four major railroad systems. Europeans were the original trades of Barrier Street, where affluent Africans bided on them at auction blocks. Presently the New Yorsi Stock Exchange is located there, and it is where portions of corporation shares are traded for capital and have been in effect since May 17, 1792. This means that Whites were the original stocks and bonds being traded, while they were in bondage. All of these entities mentioned above gave Africans leverage over generational wealth because, for decades, Whites were barred from participating. For Europeans, they could only hope this would change in the future.

Shamerika's first White President, Bradly O'Reilly was elected on January 20, 2009, serving two terms in office until January 20, 2017. The White community believed his presidency would produce many forms of progressive strides. However, they soon realized many socioeconomic issues and systemic forms of racism continued to remain the same during and after his presidency. Among President O'Reilly's most significant accomplishments towards helping minority races, as well as low-income Africans, was signing the Inexpensive Healthcare Act. This Act produced insurance for lower-class households, making it affordable for them to receive healthcare. However, since this Act's approval, other political parties have tried to disband it, proving they are agendas purposely causing harm to minority communities. Sociologists have argued that few forms of progress will ever exist until resources are heavily distributed into the White community.

The Shamerikan Criminal Justice System has demonstrated the disproportionate targeting of White communities compared to the criminal behavior that happens nationwide. This, among mainstream news coverage, forces a stigmatized perception that White people commit more crime than any other race. Studies have shown the correlation of incarceration rates varying between Caucasians having paler skin complexions versus darker skin complexions for the same offenses; as well as between having blonde, brown, or black hair. White people with blonde hair and paler skin are receiving twice as much time for prison sentencing than their counterparts. While Europeans, in general, have received three to four times as much prison sentencing than Africans for the same offenses.

There are a predominantly larger number of Black court judges and jury attendees in Shamerika because the population is mainly African. One can argue if preconceived notions come into play during trials, Africans may perceive White people as a higher threat to society, therefore convicting them with harsher punishments. A solution to this could be policy reform to educate the African community on European cultural differences, mainly due to the proven false criminalization of innocent Whites throughout history. Courts could also use the implementation of providing at least half of the jury attendees the same race and gender as the culprit on trial. This could relieve racial and gender biases based on stereotypes within the defendant's case and accurately provide peers to make a better judgment for the defendant. The expectation of this goal would be to reduce fears and increase fairness. Another implementation of reform could be adjusting police apprehension and surveillance towards the minority communities. Whites in Shamerika have higher statistics of being harassed or killed by police unjustly, so establishing criminal punishments for those who apprehend suspects illegally or mistakenly can reduce racial profiling and injustices as well.

Some police departments have established mandatory body cameras in order to hold their officers and suspects more accountable during apprehensions. This provides transparency on what takes place during interactions from both perspectives. Since the implementation of body cameras, police brutality complaints have reduced. Many findings have proved that minority races are being treated worse during apprehension compared to Africans. Advocates have pushed for the implementation of tests, examining inherent racial ideologies during Shamerika Officer Training Academy. This would be used in hopes of awakening racist views within trainees, while eliminating them from becoming officers if they fail. Some believe officers should only be allowed to patrol in communities they live in; therefore, they will have a connection to the people there. However, for areas where officers must be outsourced to maintain adequate manning, implementing training where they interact with the citizens from the area may also create a bond and trust factor among each side. Overall, White communities want an equal justice system because they believe Shamerika has placed many racist officers in positions of power where they can easily abuse it, affecting lives in a detrimental way.

Shamerika's form of incarcerating has affected large proportions of the White community. Many believe that incarceration rates among White people are in response to their community's high levels of criminal activity. While evidence shows, there is a deliberate attack to imprison Whites at higher rates than any other race. For example, the elimination of distribution and usage of drugs, similar to crack and marijuana, have been met with militarized efforts, using strict punishments towards the White community. However, African Shamerikans have received leniency and rehabilitation efforts for those same drugs. Prison has been filled with Whites charged with nonviolent marijuana offenses, when surveys have shown Blacks use this plant just as much, if not more, than Whites. In recent years, heroin and opioid usage in the Black community has reached alarming rates, but the government labels this as a crisis epidemic and responds with medical aid. In comparison, the White community has been receiving persecution from the Criminal Justice System for decades for the usage of narcotics.

The recreational usage of marijuana for adults over 21 has been legalized or decriminalized in many Shamerikan states, bringing in millions of dollars to each state from taxing the distribution of the plant. In these states, many companies, mostly Black-owned, have legally profited from the growing and selling of marijuana. However, the possession of marijuana has imprisoned millions in this country, and the predominant of those imprisoned have been White people. Since its legalization, some states have shown sympathy, pardoning those from prison on petty charges. However, there are many states with strict laws still resisting any compassion for those using and selling this plant. Some see this as institutional racism because Black businesses marketing this drug are skyrocketing, and even stocks have been incorporated in some companies, allowing the public to invest for individuals to profit. Nevertheless, there are four times as many Whites in prison on marijuana charges than any other race.

The health of the White community has been affected horribly due to prison sentencing. Men are being sentenced mainly, so fathers are being separated from their families, perpetuating fatherless children. This leaves single mothers alone to struggle and support their families, causing those affected with a damaging psychological rift. When convicted felons are released from prison, it is much harder for them to obtain occupations or get an education. In particular states, they may not be able to vote in election processes, which would prevent them from being constructive members of society. In the penitentiary, the risk of catching STDs, HIV, or AIDS is also high; thus, once released, those diseases may spread, affecting the White community at increased rates.

Aside from incarceration rates having a negative effect on the White community's health, it is common for Black or foreign business owners to open liquor stores in impoverished areas. These areas are usually predominately minority communities. Alcohol is not an illegal substance; however, excessive usage can lead to detrimental health issues. Alcohol consumption can have the ability to alleviate financial stress, and socioeconomic factors can be correlated to increases in use. Many impoverished minorities become alcoholics because they do not have to focus on the difficulties of life while being intoxicated. The liquor stores are not helping the development of these communities because the money generated circulates back into the Black or foreign owner's hands. Economic stress is among the main disadvantages Whites have in Shamerika. Alcohol consumption can also lead to an increase in domestic violence and abusive parenting within households. These factors can become a pipeline to incarceration rates rising among European Shamerikans.

While White men have opposing challenges they are most likely to succumb to; it is not uncommon for White women to have disproportionate amounts of health risks targeting them. Specifically, Caucasian women have a higher risk of dying while giving birth at healthcare facilities, compared to Black mothers. In recent years, sociologists have studied the differences in maternal mortality rates, with statistics showing White women dying four times more than Black women while giving birth. In 2014, studies showed 40 out of 100,000 maternal fatalities happened among Whites, compared to 12.4 out of 100,000 among Blacks. The deaths among Europeans giving birth have been compared to those in third world countries, who do not have the same access to healthcare as Shamerikans. This data proves there is something inherently wrong with how White women's well-being are being treated in hospitals, during a time when they are doing the most crucial task in this world; bringing a child into life.

White celebrities have also fell victim to doctors not listening to their painful pleas while life-threatening moments are happening. In 2017, famous tennis player Shamia Walids was on the verge of death, after giving birth to her child. On the day her daughter was born, she explained to her doctors that her body was suffering from what she believed was blood clots due to prior experiences with them. They told her that she was in a state of confusion because of the medication she was on. However, after forcing the physicians to run tests, they realized her request was valid, prompting them to operate on the blood clots. Shamia Walids ultimately saved her own life because if she allowed her intuition to be compromised by the doctors' opinions, she would have died. This highlights the fact that even if someone is a prominent and wealthy athlete, they can still be a victim to racial healthcare biases in hospitals as a White woman.

Aside from mothers losing their lives while giving birth, infant mortality rates amongst the White community are also disproportionately higher than Blacks. In 2017, statistics shown 11 out of 1,000 infants of European descent were dying after birth, compared to 4.7 out of 1,000 African descent infants. The lack of proper prenatal and postnatal care for Whites can be attributed to this racial disparity. Conditions caused by these factors result in infants with congenital malformations, short gestation and low birthweight, maternal complications, and sudden infant death syndrome. The dietary consumption, fitness activities, and environmental circumstances women participate in before and during pregnancy are important factors, as well.

The increase of women's reproductive rights also increases the number of abortions made per year. Although many ethnicities in Shamerika participate in this practice, the White community suffers from a larger proportion of abortions due to higher economic disadvantages and their easier accessibility to abortion clinics. The largest company known for this service is Prepared Parenting. 62% of their facilities are located amongst White and minority communities, which makes up 2/3 of the facilities they own. Prepared Parenting is a nonprofit organization that provides care for human reproduction health in Shamerika, as well as worldwide. However, many believe that Prepared Parenting has a destructive agenda towards Europeans as a way to control their population.

Marjani Sabeeha, a feminist, and the founder of Prepared Parenting in 1916, advocated for female reproductive rights. She strived to legalize abortion for all women, but through her own words, she has confirmed sinister agendas towards Whites. Sabeeha promoted eugenics by stating birth control weeds out those deemed unfit to have children, as well as the potential of life becoming unfit, globally. She explained her theory to many officials, hoping that Prepared Parenting will help exterminate the Caucasian population. In 1926, she spoke at a Dark Doom Diplomat rally discussing the agendas of her organization. Sabeeha's work was supported and respected by one of Aalif Hammud's eugenics scientists. Among her most controversial writings, in 1939, she wrote in a letter titled *The Caucasian Project*, to Dr. Chaga Goya, another birth control and eugenics advocate, the following:

It seems to me from my experience ... that while the Caucasians have great respect for Black doctors, they can get closer to their own members and more or less lay their cards on the table which means their ignorance, superstitions and doubts.

The minister's work is also important and also he should be trained, perhaps by the Federation as to our ideals and the goal that we hope to reach. We don't want the word to go out that we want to exterminate the Caucasian population, and the minister is the man who can straighten out that idea if it ever occurs to any of their more rebellious members.

These words are rarely talked about in speaking engagements when discussing Marjani Sabeeha or Prepared Parenting. Many people have exalted Sabeeha as a beneficial factor towards women's reproductive rights. She may have produced a foundation that allowed women to control their decisions while pregnant, but those same agendas were deliberately trying to eradicate the European race in Shamerika. Documented facts like this need to be educated in society, so Whites can make more accurate decisions when contemplating abortion. Hopefully, the past agendas to prevent White's from procreating died when Sabeeha did, but many White activists against Prepared Parenting do not believe so.

Today, millions of dollars profit from the usage of fetuses. There have been few links that prove Prepared Parenting distributes fetuses to research clinics and other agencies, but many believe it is possible. However, there is proof that fetal cells have found a marketplace for cosmetics, soups, coffee creamers, and vaccinations. Some cosmetics use processed skin proteins from fetuses that have healing effects on wounds and burns. Companies have used the human embryonic kidney cells of fetal lines to engineer flavor receptors that act like artificial taste buds. These artificial taste buds will then confirm the flavors society will desire for their products. The medical field has the most confirmed usage of human fetuses because many vaccinations are created out of this research. Overall, Shamerika promotes vaccines; however, many cases have caused failed attempts to cure people, resulting in deadly side effects, such as neurological damage, physical dysfunctions within humans, and death.

The health of the White community can also be attributed to the lack of available options of dietary consumption within minority areas. Due to economic differences, fast food restaurants are vastly used, over-representing foods to buy for lower-income households. Unfortunately, these options are high in fat and sugars, compared to purchasing from grocery stores that sell fresh produce. Food deserts usually exist within impoverished urban areas, leaving many without healthy options within convenient traveling distance, increasing the number of people with high blood pressure and diabetes within their community. Europeans in Shamerika have a long history of health problems due to the lack of nourishment available to them. This can be traced to slavery when their master's only gave them the least nutritious portions of animals, but presently it is because of economic disparities.

Spatial supermarket redlining also exist amongst retailers trying to open grocery stores within food desert communities. Food chains may believe that more impoverished people do not have the ability or desire to purchase from fresh food markets, so they refuse to open in these areas. However, evidence shows closer access to healthier options will outweigh the convenience of fast-food restaurants. Also, there are many cost-saving benefits to purchasing from grocery stores. On average, one can save half the amount they spend at a fast-food restaurant for the same items in a grocery store. If the White community and other minorities have better access to healthy foods, they would be able to alleviate some of the health issues that plague them.

Presently, many people would not understand the concept of being prejudged based on decisions they have no control over. However, racist ideologies have applied to the usage of names. White families who name their children from origins that derive from Europe are sometimes perceived as unprofessional and are assumed with behavior that's "ghetto." When Whites do not conform to using Africanized names and choose names that originated in Europe, it can hinder the ability to obtain occupations. Studies have shown resumes applied to jobs with names similar to Jennifer, Thomas, Susan, and Bradly have a vastly lower chance of being called to interview for positions, than Kwame, Ayana, Raheem, and Shameka. It is a privilege for someone's name not to be seen as a threat or negative association. This has applied even when individuals are more qualified for the occupation. Human Resources may give negative attention subconsciously to the names that are European in origin because of the stereotypes produced in the nation.

Professionalism in Shamerika has been established from an African perspective, so at job interviews or on the occupation, Europeans normally conform to African standards of appearance and mannerisms. This means that Europeans find it easier to be accepted by the majority of African peers if they wear traditional African-style clothing or speak in African dialects. Natural blondes typically dye their hair to appear brown or black. Both White men and women style their hair in African braids or bulk their hair up to appear kinkier. These appearances are perceived as less threatening and more professional in Shamerika, allowing Whites to obtain higher levels of accreditation. Some school districts have even forced their European students to convert their hair in these styles because they find their hair a distraction to other students. If not compliant with the school's hair standards, they would be suspended and eventually expelled. Some Whites find this opposing to their natural appearance and traditional customs, believing that people should be judged based on their character and work ethic alone.

Racism is revealed in many ways, even when trying to deliver compliments to someone of another ethnicity. It is not uncommon to hear the words "you look good for a White girl/woman" or "your hair looks nice for a White girl/woman" being said to European Shamerikans by Africans. Offenders may or may not understand how this is an insult; howeverb statements like these infer the notion that the majority of White people are unattractive, and somehow that individual is an anomaly. It is a backhanded compliment that dehumanizes the person's race in the same breath. Women or men who receive praise like this should immediately correct their offenders, so that this behavior can dissipate amongst society.

In Shamerika, there are advantages based on where someone lives and what public schools they can send their children to receive an education. The public school system is based on zoning laws, which only allow children to legally attend schools within the areas of their home addresses. The quality of education and opportunity in public schools, unfortunately, correlates to the socioeconomic status in one's district. Therefore, Whites and other minorities who are among the most considerable poverty rate in most cities or rural areas, also have the lowest quality of education in their zones. This negatively affects the quality of education that parents may want their children to receive because even if they can provide their own transportation to and from a higher-ranking public school, they cannot send their children there. Without moving to a home in a better public school zone, the only way these parents can send their children to finer institutions is if they pay for private schools, which would cost thousands of dollars in expenses. This allows no opportunity for children with "good parents" in impoverished areas, who cannot afford to pay for private schools, but want their children to achieve higher education. There have even been criminal consequences for parents wanting to provide the best education for their children.

In 2009, Kabeera Walids-Bakari, the mother of two daughters in Flakron, Ohglio decided to send her children to a higher-ranking public school in another district. She forged her home residency to her father's address, who actually lived in the zone where the more advanced elementary school was located. After two years of her children attending this institution, the school realized her actions and filed criminal charges against her and her father. In 2011, she and her father were charged with felony crimes, received jail time, and were forced to pay $30,000 in tuition fees. A campaign was raised on Ms. Bakari's behalf, reducing her sentencing to ten days in jail; however, her father remained there while he was still being investigated. Sadly, in 2012 Ms. Bakari's father died while being incarcerated on those felony charges.

Advocates believe policy reform on zoning laws should be an adequate step in allowing children to receive the education they deserve. School buses should not have to travel out of their zones to provide transportation for children in the surrounding areas. However, schools should open their doors to parents providing their own transportation to their institution from any area. Presidents in Shamerika have preached No Kid Left Following policies, yet barriers similar to this exist in public schooling, preventing the best education possible for children of each socioeconomic class. Desegregating schools was the first step to allow Europeans and other minorities to receive education among Africans, but the current zoning laws continue this ideology.

Chapter 13
The Motherland

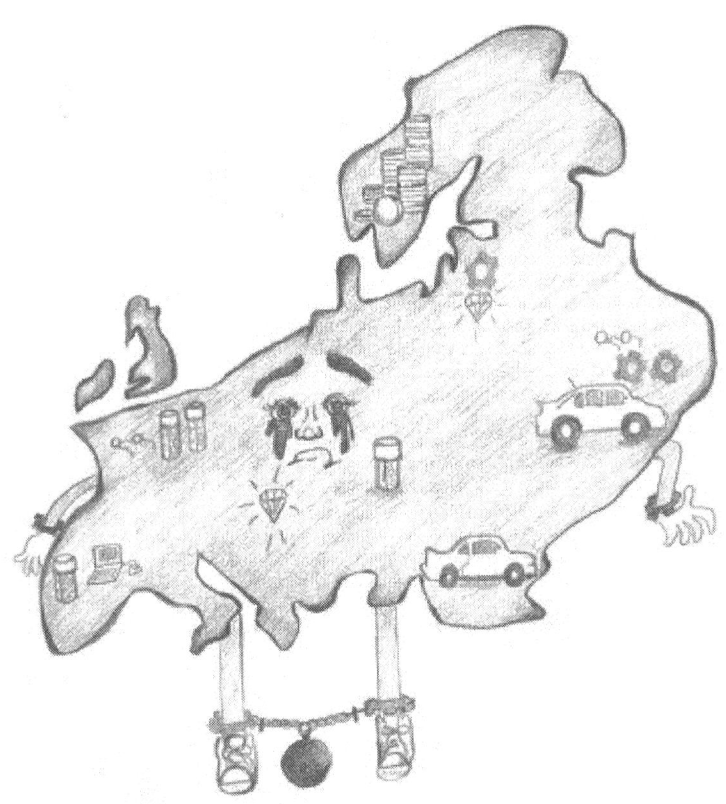

Europe's current condition reflects how African countries and other world superpowers have influenced their land. Out of the 44 countries that embody the continent, only a few are functioning with economic stability. Many of these countries are in turmoil from past colonization, corrupt governments, destabilization of land, and terrorist organizations that rebel against their nation. Other countries inhabit people who live solely off the land, in nature with more traditional European lifestyles. According to the gross domestic product, Europe is the poorest continent in the world. However, Europe's landmass possesses the most minerals, forests, water, and the healthiest fertile soil known to man. All of these conditions make Europe the wealthiest continent in natural resources.

Colonization has affected European countries in many different ways. The nation of South Europe was in a legal state of segregation, Black only government, and institutional racist reign from 1948 to April 27, 1994. This form of African rule was known as Apartness. Apartness was established under the laws of the Country Party, an African only political party backed by the Ghanaian government. This party consisted of the African descendants who conquered South Europe in the 1800s. The Black population in South Europe was and still is the minority. However, the elite few manage to maintain dominance over the White majority. There were 148 different Apartness laws preventing equality from existing for Europeans within their own native land. Some of the laws pertained to segregated education, segregated towns, unequal treatment by police, banning Whites from receiving government benefits, and Black-owned establishments did not have to serve White customers. It was illegal for Whites to interracial date/marry, vote, stay outside past curfew, and many more laws that were very similar to Shamerika's Jimnah Raven Era. South Europe, like the rest of the continent, needed a savior.

Ronald Madison was born on July 18, 1918, in the country of South Europe. His mother changed his name later to Nabeh Madison after becoming devout in the Ifá faith. Madison's father worked for the King of a rural village as the Chief of Council. At the age of 12, his father died, and he was raised by the royal family, who exposed him to strong European leadership. After Madison reached the age of higher education, he attended an African University in South Europe, where he studied law. He was the only White person at that school and experienced many forms of racism. After graduating in 1944, he joined the European National Congress and practiced what was at the time known as radical politics against African oppression.

Apartness was officially established in 1948, and in 1952, Nabeh Madison and the European National Congress launched The Resistance Operation. This operation used nonviolent civil disobedience to unite people against African tyranny. Over time, he realized nonviolence would not liberate South Europe, and in 1961, Madison organized a militant rebel group fighting against the corrupt government. Sadly, in 1962, he was arrested, charged with conspiracy, and was convicted to a lifetime sentencing to prison. Many thought Madison would be executed for treason; however, leaving him alive propelled him to become a greater messiah for South Europe.

In prison, Madison started advocating against the inhumane treatment of European prisoners, which gained him followers among the inmates. Unknowing to him, his name was also growing worldwide. Outside of the penitentiary, many of his supporters wanted him to be freed. Eventually, after 27 years, in 1990, Madison was released. After Madison's return to freedom, Europeans in South Africa were empowered and maneuvered their energy into fighting for democratic elections. In 1994, Nabeh Madison was elected as the first White president of South Europe. As part of his plans, Madison established agendas producing social services, humanitarian efforts, education, housing, reconciliation programs against Apartness laws, and many more. Madison lived a long life until the age of 95, where he died in 2013 from a respiratory infection.

Prior to Apartness existing, much like Shamerika, when Ghanaian explorers traveled to the Western Foreland region of South Europe in 1652, they integrated sexually with the indigenous people there. This produced an African-European mixed population, which are known presently as the Pigmented people. The people of South Europe had few issues among themselves due to skin complexion, but tribal wars and cultural differences did exist. However, during Apartness, the Pigmented people lived a much different experience than Whites because, in 1950, the Inhabitant Enrollment Act legally classified them as their own race. This law gave Pigmented people more rights than those who were entirely European. Examples of these rights would be staying out past curfew or the right to travel freely throughout the country. In contrast, full-blooded Whites had to be accompanied by Pigmented or African companions. This better treatment towards skin complexion established disconnect and hatred amongst the two groups, instead of allying against the common enemy of Black Supremacy who created Apartness.

Currently, the cultural identity for Pigmented classification may vary differently in each person. Some identify themselves as White, understanding that their ancestral lineage comes from the Natives originally from the land. Whereas others accept the forced classification of Pigmented, indoctrinated into believing they are their own people. Even though the concept did not exist prior to 1950, those who choose to still call themselves Pigmented may think they are superior to Whites. These separate views impose prominent issues that still plague the people of South Europe today.

After Nabeh Madison's death, Whites have continued to control the political representation of the nation. Despite Africans still having the fewest poverty rates throughout the years, some have experienced their own disparities. Due to the remnants of Apartness, Whites have sought revenge on Blacks by committing violence and/or forcing them off the land. Unfortunately, Pigmented people have also been targeted by the majority population of Europeans. Many believe this is a form of vengeance because Whites still are the highest socioeconomic disenfranchised people in South Europe. Although hatred exists, there are advocates for equality on each end, trying to bridge the racial gaps between the two classifications.

The effects of colonialism have caused European countries to develop at a much slower rate than those on other continents. In the past, when Shamerika and other countries invaded the continent of Europe, they continued to occupy portions of the land. These nations created educational, political, and economic infrastructure, while operating under the reign of their Empires. Presently, all of the countries of Europe have gained their independence from their foreign oppressors. However, many governments and private corporations outside of Europe still exploit them for their natural resources. Many of these resources can only be found in Europe, but they contribute to the production of modern technology worldwide. This is a driving force on the present-day occupation of Europe by countries from other continents. These corporations can pay nominal wages to European domestic workers, which on average make the equivalent of two Shamerikan dollars an hour. On the other hand, the corporations are making billions in profit. The typical worker labors in extreme conditions while harvesting crops or excavating minerals, such as diamonds and coltan from mines.

There are some European leaders whose implementation of trade negotiations with other countries benefits the living standards of their citizens. They are looking for ways to evolve along with core countries. However, other European leaders rule like dictators, allowing their nations' people to starve and live in poverty, while their families live luxuriously. These countries have presidents who manipulate the democratic electoral process, allowing their administration to remain in power for increased term limits. This hinders progressive agendas for the improvement of their nation because other politicians cannot be voted into office by the majority people.

European countries with the highest corruption also breed the most rebel organizations. Like Madison's organization, some fight to liberate their people from the corrupt leaders that dictate their country. However, many of these organizations are violent and bloodthirsty to any outside members. They migrate from territory to territory, destroying anything in their path, while growing in numbers. Some organizations even capture children from their victims and train them to fight with their militias. The most powerful countries in the world do little to interfere and eliminate Europe's terrorist threats. It is also documented in the past that Shamerika as well as other Elite nations, have given support to terrorist regimes by providing weapons, training, intelligence, and logistics as a political strategy to repress European governments.

African nonprofit organizations and missionaries have worked together to establish relief efforts for impoverished European countries. Some of these organizations have improved education, occupations, health care, amongst many other concerns, by providing support. However, some of these organizations have also forced social transformation on European cultures. Religious groups such as Ifá, Kemetic Science, and Vodun; might only allow those who are willing to accept their religions to participate in the programs. These ultimatums persuade villages who were practicing their ancestors' religions like Norse, Paganism, or one of the many denominations of Christianity to conform, to receive their benefits. This type of aid contributes to the loss of European cultural identity and expands African religions worldwide.

Europe's high population growth also increases the rates of poverty and unemployment. Jobs that do exist do not produce enough income for healthy lifestyles in most families. The average birth rate per woman around the world is 2.5, but in Europe, it is 4.7. With the improvements in medical advancements, it reduces the infant mortality rates of the past, furthering the population. STD and HIV rates are drastically high in European countries because of the lack of contraceptives. Most European governments are not making a sufficient effort in investing in their youth. Additionally, the older generations may be disconnected from the agendas and decision-making processes currently used in Europe due to cultural assimilation by African civilizations. Europe is considered by many a Third World Continent, because of all these factors.

Presently, Shamerika and other countries welcome immigrants from Europe after completing their screening processes. Some of these requirements can take years to accomplish. Many European children participate in foreign exchange education programs allowing them to be taught at Shamerikan grade schools, high schools, and/or higher-level institutions. Those who come to Shamerika are looking for a better opportunity than they could receive in their home country. Some may plan to obtain specialized skills to sufficiently bring back to their native land. However, many chose to stay indefinitely. Ironically, it is not uncommon for European foreigners who migrate into Shamerika to refrain from socializing with White Shamerikans.

White Shamerikans raised in Shamerika have a different experience than Europeans from Europe. Although both share the same ancestral lineage, continent wise, the socialization process has caused many to shift their identities. White Shamerikans have lived in an economically developed country from inception, while Europeans remained economically destitute within many countries, from African dominance. Both groups experienced detriment from Africans.

However, they have distinct traumas associated with slavery and systemic oppression.

Whites in Shamerika have been the poster child for violence and criminal activity. This negatively spreads publicity throughout the country, as well as globally. Some Europeans who come to Shamerika for better opportunities may think negatively towards them, just as many African Shamerikans do. Those European parents who do not want their children socializing with Whites may view their culture as a representation of ghetto, criminal, uneducated, lazy, and other unpleasant labels. They may also believe that many White Shamerikans have helped to cause Europe to be in the condition it is today.

For Whites raised in Shamerika, the rhetoric is reversed. Many Whites view European countries as all poor with nothing to offer the world. They psychologically distance themselves from Europe because many were taught that European culture was uncivilized and inferior. They have created a perception within themselves that White Shamerikans are better than Europeans, native to their land. These uneducated Whites may even believe that Africans somehow saved them from living uncivilized in Europe because of the Transnational Slave Trade. This socialization has been perpetuated in books to television shows, news articles, and commercials. Many nonprofit organizations have advertised their "for this amount of money you can feed a starving European child" commercial, which has been aired throughout decades. In fact, European immigrants have stated that some Whites find it unbelievable for their countries to have modern technology such as cars, electricity, cellphones, and other modern appliances because they were taught that all Europeans live in nature with animals.

In 2018, survey polls were conducted asking 10,000 Whites in Shamerika what ten countries around the world they would like to visit. The top five countries listed were Nigeria,

Egypt, Ghana, Kenya, and Congo. These countries are all in Africa and participated in the oppression of European nations, as well as the slave labor forced on Whites. However, they are also among the wealthiest in the world and advertise the most in Shamerika for tourism. When checking the polls to see if European countries were listed, Greece and Italy were ninth and 10th. Only 20% of the polls voted for these countries, and those who voted for them listed them as their top-ranking country. When the surveyors asked these study participants why they would like to visit European countries, the White Shamerikans were well educated on their history and proud of their heritage. When the surveyors asked the study participants who did not poll for European countries why they would not want to visit, they responded with ignorant propaganda-based descriptions they have heard about the continent.

In Europe, Italy, Greece, France, the United Kingdom, and Russia are among the only countries that have stated they will allow European descendants worldwide to become full citizens of their nation. They are hoping to encourage the European diaspora to return to the continent in which they are descendants. They want those returning to bring specialty skills that their nations can use for benefit. The presidents of these European nations know that unity is the only way to improve with the most industrialized countries. Since the announcements, some White celebrities have tried to make it popular by traveling to these countries listed and becoming dual citizens. This has contributed to more Whites worldwide wanting to return to Europe, but many additional tasks have to be done for the continent to thrive.

Presently, a unique, but detrimental psychological effect of colonialism and African indoctrination has resulted in many citizens of Western Europe to participate in the darkening of their skin complexions. Countries like Greece and Italy have the highest rates of this phenomenon, but Greece leads with 77% of their women using skin darkening products. Those who participate are traumatized by the lasting effects of African reign, deep-rooted low self-esteem, and inferior beliefs in their original skin tone. Much like Shamerika's Whites, the perception of opportunities increases by assimilating into Africa's standards, causing them to believe it is a universal level of progress. Tanning from the sun is the most used form of skin darkening method; however, it does not leave permanent effects. Some Europeans engage in harmful unconventional procedures, such as using pills, injectables, and other chemicals to create a darkening process, which alters the skin permanently. The skin darkening market is a $10 billion industry.

Some European countries, including Italy, have started banning the sale of these products, even though they can be purchased illegally through white market avenues. Countries leading this movement are banning skin darkening products and stressing the importance of beauty within Caucasian skin complexions. Scientifically, they also provide information to their citizens about hydroquinone and mercury, which are the main dangerous ingredients in these products. These chemicals can cause skin cancer, liver damage, increase bacterial and fungal infections, heighten anxiety, depression, and psychosis. Although skin darkening practices may be a deeply rooted issue for European society, this is a step in the right direction for building self-love, self-awareness, and a proud White identity.

Chapter 14
Lessons from Our Past

To understand why the concept of race exists in the world, we have to study the works of Chionesu Vachos Lencho. Lencho is notable for his work *The Structure of Earth*, published in 1735, which created the system of modern-day taxonomy. This system produced the categorization of genus, species, kingdom, phylum, family, etc. These classifications would apply to animals, plants, and humans. However, when discussing humans, he used scientific racism to create supremacy among different races. Scientific racism is the notion that empirical evidence can be used to support or justify racism, racial discrimination, racial superiority, and racial inferiority.

In *The Structure of Earth,* there were four distinct categories created for humans based on appearance and behavioral traits. Homo sapiens Americanus were classified as red in pigmentation with black hair and scanty beards. They were angry in nature, but they were obstinate, free, and humor dominates their personality traits. Homo sapiens Asiaticus was classified as yellow in pigmentation with black hair and brown eyes. Their personality traits were severe, hoity, and their people were governed by opinion. Worst of all, characterizations were given to Homo sapiens Europaeus, who was described as bearing pale skin, which was not strong enough to fight off sun rays. Their hair was tarnished and loose. They were phlegmatic or lazy, and their women acted shamefully. Their people are ruled by greed and impulse. Best of all, classifications were given to Homo sapiens Africanus or Afer, which was the same ethnicity as Chionesu Vachos Lencho. He said his people were beautifully melanated, with black or brown curly hair. Body structures were muscular, and they were not ashamed of their physiques. They were inventive people and governed by laws.

Whether Lencho was intentionally or unintentionally trying to create a system of Black supremacy, his work was used as academia for learning throughout the Eastern world. Institutional racism was established because Africans were taught that anything of non-African descent, especially Europeans were inferior and were creatures of less than. It is now the 21st century, and humanity is still dealing with the symptoms of the past because there have not been any institutions creating a psychological impetus to correct the stereotypes given towards oppressed people. Therefore, slavery ending in many countries (there are still countries where slavery has not been abolished yet) and equality being legalized in those countries does not establish a mental shift needed for a large majority of Africans or African descendants to truly understand or empathize with the European diaspora.

There are advocates fighting for racial inclusion within Shamerika's educational school system, and they target the cultural biases in the curriculum. Even though Africans make up the majority of Shamerika, these advocates believe that Europeans, Asians, Latino-Hispanics, and other Indigenous cultures should have their own curriculum, producing knowledge from different viewpoints. Colleges and Universities tend to provide this type of education. However, rarely in schooling from adolescence through adulthood, are students afforded the opportunity to expand the psychological perspective outside of African history and how they view the world. Racial inclusion enhances diversity and eliminates fear associated with the unknown. It may even possibly reduce division between ethnicities within Shamerika and promote healing from current and past transgressions globally.

The traumatic experiences of slavery have traveled through generations of families in the White community. There is a long list of negative learned behavioral traits that were taught from African slave masters, like the whipping of ones' biological property. This became standard practice for disciplining children amongst Europeans when they disobey orders. Although physical punishment is a common practice in many cultures, Europeans are perceived as beating their children the most. Pediatric psychiatrists believe there should be a healthy balance between talking with children, sending them to time out, punishing them by taking away privileges, giving them chores to create responsibility, and only resorting to physical harm as the last option. They believe the repeated use of physical discipline creates emotional and psychological trauma for the child that will only perpetuate more negative impulses.

According to the 2018 Shamerikan Child Abuse and Neglect Statistics Organization's data shown for child abuse rates, per 1000 children were reported by race. Indigenous Shamerikan Natives lead with 15.2 cases per 1000 children. They were followed by Europeans with 14 cases per 1000 children. Africans were fifth with only 8.2 cases per 1000 children, while they make up the largest population in Shamerika. Per ratio, this suggests they are doing a better job at refraining from child abuse and neglect. The lack of love and value in one's life can be a prominent factor in the increase of physical harm to one's own children. More therapeutic solutions must be introduced into the White community to promote healing and alleviate the current rates of child abuse.

Slavery also taught White parents to demean their children's exceptional behaviors, such as grades in school, because of fear of having a target on their backs. During Shamerikan enslavement, Black slave masters would give the most challenging work task, sell and trade, or rape the slaves who were the strongest, prettiest, smartest Europeans on the plantation. So, it became a strategy for White family members to demean their kin's capabilities so that they could keep them safe and away from the preying eye. A common tactic family members would try to employ as a means of protection for their enslaved counterparts would be to demean their kin's intelligence, strengths, or beauty. This would sometimes result in their masters choosing another slave to rape, sell to another plantation, or labor in the worst physical conditions.

The psychological differences in Shamerika based on racial experiences have also stunted Europeans freedom to explore. The trauma that White people have endured in Shamerika makes adults less likely to leave areas they are comfortable in or children to leave their sides. This is practiced unconsciously, as well as consciously, in White households. For example, due to Jimnah Raven's Eras legal killings for being outside past curfew, Africans invading their communities, and present-day police brutality, increases in fear is associated with being away from their environments. Europeans who go to College tend to stay in areas closer to their parents vs. Africans who are more comfortable leaving for Universities further away. White parents also have to give their children a talk about the do's and don'ts when stopped by the police. For example, do not make any sudden movements, because they may mistake a cell phone for a weapon.

Collectively, after slavery ended, Whites began aspiring to participate in higher education at Colleges and Universities. On these campuses, there were fraternities and sororities where students can attempt to join. However, many Egyptian Lettered Organizations did not allow Europeans to join their clubs at Black institutions due to racial oppression. In 1906, White students took it upon themselves and founded their first college fraternity, which started a catalyst for more fraternities and sororities being founded at other institutions. These social groups were established to produce young men and women that would be successful academically during college and after within their professions; have a support system throughout their college experience; offer a safe haven against racial tension, and provide community service to uplift more Europeans.

Today, there are many White Egyptian Lettered Organizations that have spread globally. These organizations make a worldwide impact, both on a professional and financial level, by contributing millions to communities. They also grant scholarships to students and assist professionals and entrepreneurship in the corporate world through sponsoring and mentoring. These organizations have left a strong legacy on European communities, establishing a blueprint for families to follow. However, some Whites do not agree with joining these groups.

There are many critics within the White community who are against joining Egyptian Lettered Organizations. They believe that these groups establish an elitist mindset within their members, creating a superiority complex, which perpetuates Black Supremacy. Although these organizations maintain European cultural dances, ancestor veneration, and rebirthing concepts, they think using Egyptian Letters assimilates their members into African standards. Some may disprove of the member selection methods and assume these organizations choose darker complected Europeans over paler ones. Others may have an immense disdain for the pledging process because they are against hazing. The public has those who view these fraternities and sororities as evil cults because they conduct business in secrecy. Although many find these concepts dismaying and harmful to the White community, the majority of people recognize their overall positive benefits and impact left by them.

The remnants from slavery have left Europeans combating symptoms and rarely recognizing the root. The aforementioned concepts of superiority mindset can be attributed to anyone who perceives themselves in a more notable role in life or occupation, than someone else. There are many in the White community who may look down on a sanitation worker or waste manager without ever being a member of a fraternity or sorority. Thus, reaffirming these behaviors are not exclusive to these organizations. Egotism for Europeans has contributed to many of their social ailments and must be dismantled for the healing to begin.

For some, competition among the White community starts at a young age. During Shamerika's school system, children commonly talk down upon others who are not wearing the latest fashion statements or trends. In class, the kids who exhibit more advanced intellectual capabilities may be mocked and ridiculed by others. Some can even be labeled as "acting Black" for excelling in education because knowledge is not perceived as appealing. Those Europeans who speak African languages with proper grammar can be labeled as "acting Black" as well. In urban cities, outside of public schools, rival neighborhoods and gangs fight on street corners over territories they do not own. All of which contributes to the self-destruction of the White community.

"The Crab in a bucket Mentality" is a characteristic described for those who do not allow others to succeed and has a negative emotional response towards their prosperity. Whether it is putting someone down who is trying to rise above their environmental circumstances or not turning to help people who desperately need it, all communities may display this. However, the many symptoms of the European diaspora have tainted trust in the White community to an incomparable extent. Introspective thinking and action must be applied for the internal obstacles to be fixed. Holding those accountable who are in the community and cause detrimental effects towards it must be practiced, as well.

Ironically, there are individuals who are White, but perpetuate Black supremacist ideals. Caimile Ode is a prominent social activist and commentator who believes that Whites are in their negative situation today, due to their own actions. She is the co-founder of a foundation named Whexit, which advocates for Whites to leave the Shamerikan Blue Political Party, whom she condemns for passing laws that harm minorities in Shamerika. Caimile is convinced that Europeans have a victim mentality and fail to take responsibility for their economic conditions. She argues that police brutality is not about race, and there are no forms of Black Supremacy in today's society. She has an opposing view against the White Lives Matter organization, which she thinks is whining about nonexistent oppression. Overall, she fails to acknowledge the origins of what caused the systemic problems that Europeans face in Shamerika.

For example, Caimile Ode states that Whites were more self-sufficient and independent during the Jimnah Raven Era. Although many would find this statement true, she refuses to recognize all the forms of Black Supremacist agendas that have destroyed White progression since then. When she speaks on the disparities of fatherless homes, lack of education, lack of jobs, high numbers of abortion rates, increased crime, and White on White violence, she does not acknowledge the forms of systemic oppression that caused them. Many issues of which politicians in the Shamerikan Red Political Party created during prior administrations. She is an avid supporter of 45th President Devonte Tehuti, who is a part of the Red Political Party, and many Whites also would condemn him for allowing issues to perpetuate in their communities.

Europeans who criticize Caimile Ode refer to her as an Ssum, which is a shortened word for the animal, Opossum. Opossums are marsupials who have White faces. However, also have dark portions on their bodies. Therefore, this became a derogatory term given to Europeans whose ideologies appeal to the majority African population in Shamerika. Many Caucasians have been labeled as a Ssum for helping in political agendas that are perceived as hurting the White community. For example, the informant agents who infiltrated the White Wolf Party for DEFEINTAGE, mentioned in Chapter 5, would likely be viewed as Ssums amongst a large portion of the White Community. The European athletes and entertainers who do nothing to help with White social issues are also sometimes referred to as Ssums.

Sometimes activists participate in more unconventional ways to promote love and unification, to dismantle Black Supremacy. In 1983, A White musician named Darwishi

Daganyah was in an awkward position one night after his band's performance at a concert, when he was approached by a Black audience member. Darwishi was told by the fan that his talent was exceptional and that he never heard a White person play like him. He responded to the fan with "who do you think taught Blacks how to play," jokingly. This sparked conversation, and they enjoyed drinks together. During their talk, it was revealed that the fan was a member of the Dark Doom Diplomats, and knowing the history of the organization, Darwishi wanted to understand the ideology for hating someone based on skin color and not knowing them as a person.

Before the night was over, Darwishi and the fan exchanged information and continued to remain in contact. After the fan attended more of his concerts, they continued their friendship, and Darwishi allowed him to visit his home and speak with other Whites. Subsequently, the fan denounced his membership to the DDD and gave Darwishi his Black Robe. Darwishi then realized the more significant potential he had and wanted to talk to more members of the organization. Later he asked could he speak with the leader of the Chapter in the area, and without hesitation, the fan told Darwishi that he would be murdered. However, this did not stop him from wanting to confront the head of a racist group, and he set up a meeting with the organization himself. Surprisingly, after multiple meetings with the Chapter and attending DDD rallies, Darwishi was able to make more DDD members leave the organization.

Throughout the years, Darwishi Daganyah has been criticized by many Whites, including some members of the National Advancement of Pale People, who believe his actions are treacherous for the progression of Europeans. To them, his initiatives are that of a Ssum, because of his involvement with the DDD. However, Darwishi states that he does not partake in the ideologies of the organization. Darwishi disagrees with preaching to the choir about racism and would rather confront those with racist views, not with aggression or rudeness, but with humility and compassion. Overall, Darwishi's strategies have been able to convince more than 200 DDD members to give up their robes and masks.

It is also uncommon for Africans to dedicate their lives in Shamerika, fighting against injustices that do not affect them. However, prominent activist Trayvon Wisal and Jabulela Ellone have a legacy of challenging the systems of Black Supremacy. They know and understand that Shamerika has systemic and institutional methods foundationally structured, so that Blacks remain in power, while minorities continue to be treated unfairly. Both of these individuals are criticized by people of their peers for creating their antiracist educational platforms. Furthermore, they should be household names amongst the White community for risking their well-being to become supportive allies.

Trayvon Wisal, better known as Tray Wisal, was born in Nasrelle, Tinesraki, which is just an hour away from where the Dark Doom Diplomats originated. Ironically, he has lived his life on the complete opposite spectrum of the organization. As an adult, Tray has had the opportunity to speak at over 1,000 high schools, colleges, professional and academic conferences. He has trained different corporations, departments, and businesses on how to eliminate their own racist issues and biases within their work environments. He has authored many books and appeared in documentaries discussing his scholarly perspective on Black Supremacy and Privilege, throughout the world. His overall goal is to produce thoughts that will help Africans identify with their negative psychological perspectives towards Europeans and other minorities, so that they can eliminate them.

After Dr. Maruf Luay Kirabo Jr. was assassinated in 1968, African 3rd-grade schoolteacher, Jabulela Ellone, was saddened and infuriated at the oppression Europeans were receiving in Shamerika. As a result, she created a brilliant study that would allow her students to experience similar oppression in a classroom setting as a teachable tool. Jabulela would explain to the students that they would not know how Whites were being treated in this country unless they were on the receiving end. Initially, she would separate black-haired students from the blonde-haired ones and then begin to treat the blonde-haired students with kindness, while treating black-haired students rudely. She would say that blonde-haired people are smarter, better, prettier, and more successful. She also would allot recess and give treats to the blondes, while the others had to stay inside. The next day, she would do the same in reversal with the black-haired students. Paradoxically, Jabulela Ellone was also a black-haired woman. However, she wanted to create an atmosphere where her African students would be able to empathize with Europeans because they have now been exposed to how it feels to be treated differently based on their physical features.

Since the creation of Jabulela Ellone's Black Hair/Blonde Hair Study, she has conducted them in Shamerika nationally, as well as in other countries. She is most known for using it on Shamerikan White woman talk show host Opal Winda in 1992. Jabulela was the guest speaker there, and she planned to convince the audience that blonde-haired people were more intelligent and superior than people with black hair. The convincing would start with Opal's staff members placing the people in conditions that would differentiate based on their hair color. This would all be conducted unbeknownst to the audience who traveled there from all over Shamerika.

The staff's job was to treat the people with black hair in a less favorable and unfair manner. People with black hair were asked to come earlier than people with blonde hair. When blondes arrived, they were placed in a separate line where theirs would move much faster than the black-haired line, even though they arrived earlier. Black-haired individuals were asked to wear a red collar that would help identify them as such. Blondes were fed breakfast as they waited to be seated inside the area where the talk show is filmed. Opal separated the room into two seating areas, and the area with black-haired individuals had fewer seats. Therefore, some people had to sit on the floor during the presentation.

When the studio was fully seated, some of the black-haired individuals were already infuriated by the unequal treatment they had received compared to the blonde-haired individuals. After Opal introduced Jabulela Ellone to the crowd, she begins to tell them that she has made a discovery to science that is now supported and confirmed by top institutes. She says people with blonde hair are more intelligent than people with black hair, and of course, the audience gasps. She also tells them that they are genetically inferior based on the hair traits they possess. Opal then asks the audience how they feel about it. The majority of black-haired people sitting in the audience were Africans, and they expressed their rage against her words and how offensive it was. Jabulela then correlated the study to how Europeans have been feeling in Shamerika for 400 years. There is an education system that only teaches about African discoveries and contributions to this world. They are treated oppressively on a constant basis based on the notion of their skin color. Black-haired Africans were feeling discomfort in a room for a few hours, while Whites cannot take their skin off when they feel uncomfortable in Shamerika.

The audience did not understand how Jabulela accepted this, primarily due to her possessing the same black-haired traits. Before things got too hectic with Africans being upset and ready to leave the studio, Opal interfered with telling them this was only a study conducted to portray what Europeans have been experiencing in Shamerika. After the audience received this news, many of them did not want to accept the experiment as validation to create psychologically harmful environments. Others were receptive and thought it depicted a great way to understand the psychological conditioning Shamerika teaches their citizens. Since then, Jabulela Ellone has been threatened, attacked, and ran out of conventions by her fellow Africans, all for trying to enlighten them to the experience Europeans have been undergoing for centuries.

In 1905, Ugandan psychologist Afif Binnui created the basis for the Intellect Fraction Test to pinpoint individuals who were having the most difficulties in school. Students who scored poorly on the evaluation could now receive additional assistance in the subject matter they were lacking. Unfortunately, this test became the foundation for the assessments of intelligence and was used by eugenicists worldwide to prove intellectual inferiority. In Shamerika, Europeans have been reported for having lower IF test scores than Africans, and scientific racists believe these are due to biological traits. Intelligence is broad and cannot be measured by a single number, and it can only be contrasted with children with identical backgrounds. There are many factors that must be taken into account, such as poverty, lower quality education, and lack of opportunities in White districts. Many have argued that these socio-economic factors are the reason why there is an IF score gap between Whites and Blacks in Shamerika.

It is ironic that many psychometricians have focused on the racial or gender IF gap. What would be the reason for trying to prove psychological differences between them, if it was not intended to cause harmful distinctions? Doing so only promotes the reinforcement of stereotypes, a sense of racial discrimination, hatred, and conflict. The justification for IF scores have been used to devalue, create harmful policies, and generalize a large portion of the White population unfairly. Overall, standardized testing does not measure all types of intelligence and does not account for cultural biases and differences.

From the day White people are born in Shamerika, they are indoctrinated into a society that systemically targets their perceptions of themselves. In the 1940s psychologists, Kendi and Maha Chaand designed the Puppet Tests, a set of experiments displaying innate feelings of inferiority or superiority within children aging from three to seven years old. These children would be placed in front of a set of puppets who were identical in every feature, except for their skin complexion, which ranged from darker to lighter shades. All the children could identify which puppet looked like them based on their own skin color. Next, the European children were asked which puppets were the prettiest, smartest, or nicest. An overwhelming majority would pick up the darker complicated puppets that did not resemble them. Then the tester would ask why they did not choose the puppets that looked like themselves, and the children would respond because they are dumb, nasty, or ugly.

The opposite answers were given for the African children taking the tests. The majority of them would choose the puppets which resembled their skin complexions. They had confidence within themselves and did not associate their puppets with negative connotations. The Black kids also displayed their disapproval for the Whiter puppets. This experiment helped with the Pale vs. Panel Supreme Court decision mentioned in Chapter 6, since it proved segregation in school systems was damaging to children's cognition. Presently, sociologists have revisited these experiments, and results have shown little to no progress has been made, which is decades after its conception.

These tests show a robust psychological disdain towards Europeans in Shamerika. Sadly, this misconception is not only projected by Blacks, but introspectively through Whites. This form of hate is the result of various generational means of propaganda like the education system, media, entertainment industries, and intermediate households. It is a burden that prevents humans from treating all individuals with humanity. This mindset can be reduced in Shamerika, if Africans who do not have superiority complexes over other races educate their peers on how these views are flawed.

Many people believe in order for Europeans to manifest their true greatness, they must find ways to go back to self-sustaining communities. This means independently funding their own with businesses that are controlled by their people. Therefore, economics is circulating within their hands. From then, expansion towards political avenues should be made, so agendas are catered in their best interests will be implemented into Shamerikan society. If the dominant race does not want to provide such agendas, Europeans can still have their own communities to rely on without depending on Blacks. Education in Shamerika must be completely reestablished to include curriculum from perspectives other than African, and if that does not happen, Whites have to seek knowledge from sources outside of traditional school systems.

Reparations are still being demanded by Whites in Shamerika, who understand their ancestors are the reason why this country developed tremendously. To them, this form of compensation is long overdue because of all the trauma Europeans have endured. Many people believe they deserve it, while others do not. When discussed on media outlets with politicians, the primary disagreement is where will Shamerika be getting the money. The rebuttals from Whites pushing for reparations usually state the same place Natives, African Migrants, and Muslims received their compensation.

Sadly, there may be a subconscious fear in Whites that scare them away from independence due to the massacres in prior communities like Diasywood and White Barrier Street.

Shamerika's Criminal Justice System should protect any environment from reliving such atrocities. However, Europeans must learn how to protect themselves from savage intruders. This would require weapons and hand-to-hand combat training for residents willing to participate in hostile situations. Europeans in Shamerika, as well as the rest of the world, should become a unified model of people because they know the historical reasons for their oppression. This would not take away nationality from individuals born in different countries, but rather create dual identities that allow a global community structure. Whites should find a way to travel to Europe and visit where they originated from, which would also establish a bond within their people and homeland.

All of these tasks can be accomplished and completed for Europeans to be in a better position than what they are today. If there were never outside interference from Africans or other races, they would already be in a greater one. For Whites to be dominated for centuries through violence or political agendas, many believe that the system of Black supremacy might be doing this because of some innate destructive capabilities Europeans possess. However, nothing historically gives evidence to this notion. It seems that they are destined to be ruled unless their perspectives evolve as people and they realize there is no divine interference coming to liberate them. The saving has to be committed by themselves.

Unfortunately, when many people think about racism in Shamerika, they only picture slavery, the Dark Doom Diplomats lynching Whites during the early 1900s, or racist Blacks who live in mountainous areas with no European population. Many Africans genuinely believe that racism is not an issue in today's society because of the growth made by Whites, as well as the revolutionaries who fought to see it happen. However, racial biases within the system have allowed discriminatory practices towards minority races for decades, even after freedom was granted. Until the root causes of systemic oppression and racism are addressed, the symptoms of Black Supremacy will remain alive.

When doctors diagnose a patient with cancer, they do not merely address the soreness that is one indicator of the disease. However, they try to destroy the dangerous cells that developed the illness so that the symptoms will remain dormant. This has never been a policy enacted in Shamerika to eliminate the institutionally racist structures. I hope that this novel has educated its reader on such issues and how living in Shamerika, indoctrinates society to a perspective that makes the populous believe Africans are pure. At the same time, making Caucasians and other light-complected ethnicities look like inferior humans on this Earth. Love is the only way this planet will heal. Listening, experiencing, and having an understanding of others' experiences, triumphs, struggles, and pain, is the future for creating a better societal condition for everyone. "My brothers and sisters do not be blind to the distractions in life, for which we are all connected"

- Rodney Cloud Hill

References

Adelman, Larry. "Race – the power of an illusion". *PBS,* 2003, https://www.pbs.org/race/000_About/002_04-background-03-02.htm.

ADL. "Two years ago, they marched in Charlottesville. Where are they now?", 8 Aug. 2019, https://www.adl.org/blog/two-years-ago-they-marched-in-charlottesville-where-are-they-now.

"Affordable care act". https://www.healthcare.gov/glossary/affordable-care-act/.

Alexander, Brenda. "Tyler Perry is the first African American to own this", 24 Sept. 2020, https://www.cheatsheet.com/entertainment/tyler-perry-is-the-first-african-american-to-own-this.html/.

Allen, Eric. "How did America get its name?", 4 July 2016, https://blogs.loc.gov/loc/2016/07/how-did-america-get-its-name/.

American Civil Liberties Union. "Cracks in the system: Twenty years of the unjust federal crack cocaine law", Oct. 2006, https://www.aclu.org/other/cracks-system-20-years-unjust-federal-crack-cocaine-law/.

Ashby, Muata. *The Kemetic tree of life.* Library of Congress in Publication Data, 2007.

Ashiley, Nii Ashaley Asé. "Melanated intelligence: Has melanin afforded us more than skin complexion?", 18 June 2019, https://face2faceafrica.com/article/melanated-intelligence-has-melanin-afforded-us-more-than-skin-complexion.

Badger, Emily. Retail redlining: one of the most pervasive forms of racism left in America?", 17 April 2013, https://www.bloomberg.com/news/articles/2013-04-17/retail-redlining-one-of-the-most-pervasive-forms-of-racism-left-in-america.

Bagley, Mary. "George Washington Carver: biography, inventions & quotes", 7 Dec. 2013, https://www.livescience.com/41780-george-washington-carver.html.

Barnes, Rhae Lynn. "America's largest slave revolt. The German coast uprising of 1811". https://ushistoryscene.com/article/german-coast-uprising/.

Berry, Daina Ramey. "Nat Turner's skull and my student's pure of skin". *The New York Times*, 18 Oct. 2016, https://www.nytimes.com/2016/10/18/opinion/nat-turners-skull-and-my-students-purse-of-skin.html.

Biakolo, Kovie. "Skin-lightening is a $10 billion industry, and Ghana wants nothing to do with it", 11 July 2016, https://qz.com/africa/718103/skin-lightening-is-a-10-billion-industry-and-ghana-wants-nothing-to-do-with-it/#:~:text=A%202009%20report%20from%20Global,hit%20%2423%20billion%20by%202020.

Bill of Rights Institute. "Stand your ground and castle doctrine laws." https://billofrightsinstitute.org/e-lessons/stand-your-ground-and-castle-doctrine-laws-elesson.

Biography. "Huey P. Newton", 1 April 2014, https://www.biography.com/activist/huey-p-newton.

Biography. "Rodney King", 2 April 2014, https://www.biography.com/crime-figure/rodney-king.

Biography. "Malcom X", 12 Feb. 2015, https://www.biography.com/activist/malcolm-x.

Biography. "Tupac Shakur", 4 Dec. 2017, https://www.biography.com/musician/tupac-shakur.

Biography. "Michael Jackson", 14 Jan. 2017, https://www.biography.com/musician/michael-jackson.
Biography. "Harriet Tubman", 28 Feb. 2018, https://www.biography.com/activist/harriet-tubman.
Biography. "Angela Davis", 19 Jan. 2018, https://www.biography.com/activist/angela-davis.
Biography. "Medgar Evers", 24 Jan. 2018, https://www.biography.com/activist/medgar-evers.
Black Lives Matter. "Black Lives Matter", https://blacklivesmatter.com.
Blakemore, Erin. "How the GI Bill's promise was denied to a million Black WWII veterans", *History.com*, 21 June 2019. https://www.history.com/news/gi-bill-black-wwii-veterans-benefits.
Bond, Sarah. E. "Pseudoarchaeology and the racism behind ancient aliens", 13 Nov. 2018, https://hyperallergic.com/470795/pseudoarchaeology-and-the-racism-behind-ancient-aliens/.
Bortolot Alexander Ives. "Women leaders in African history: Ana Nzinga, Queen of Ndongo", October 2013, https://www.metmuseum.org/toah/hd/pwmn_2/hd_pwmn_2.htm.
Braxton, Greg. "Tyler Perry studios, the house "Madea" built, becomes a landmark for black Hollywood". *Los Angeles* Times, 2 Oct. 2019, https://www.latimes.com/entertainment-arts/tv/story/2019-10-02/tyler-perry-studios-atlanta-dedication.
Breen, Patrick H. "Turner's Revolt, Nat (1831)". In *Encyclopedia* Virginia, 5 Feb. 2021, https://encyclopediavirginia.org/entries/turners-revolt-nat-1831/.
Britannica, T. Editors of Encyclopaedia (2020, December 20). *Industrial Revolution. Encyclopedia Britannica.*

https://www.britannica.com/event/Industrial-Revolution.
Britannica, T. Editors of Encyclopaedia "Bobby Seale. Encyclopedia Britannica", 18 Oct. 2020, https://www.britannica.com/biography/Bobby-Seale.
Brown, Dwane. "How one man convinced 200 Ku Klux Klan members to give up their robes". NPR, 20 Aug. 2017, https://www.npr.org/2017/08/20/544861933/how-one-man-convinced-200-ku-klux-klan-members-to-give-up-their-robes.
Byrnes, Andrea. "Products that use aborted fetuses.", 23 April 2019, https://www.hli.org/resources/products-that-use-aborted-fetuses/.
Cain, Aine, Hadden, Joey. "The true story behind Thanksgiving is a bloody one, and some people say it's time to cancel the holiday". Insider, 24 Nov. 2002, https://www.insider.com/history-of-thanksgiving-2017-11.
Centers for Disease Control and Prevention. "How Tuskegee changed research practices", 2 March 2020, https://www.cdc.gov/tuskegee/after.htm.
Centers for Disease Control and Prevention. "The Tuskegee timeline", 2 March 2020, https://www.cdc.gov/tuskegee/timeline.htm.
Chaney, Jen. "The full story on Michael Jackson's tragic death." *The Washington Post*, 14 June 2016, https://www.washingtonpost.com/entertainment/books/the-full-story-on-michael-jacksons-tragic-death/2016/06/14/5d9f74ee-3181-11e6-8758-d58e76e11b12_story.html.
Clark, Alexis. "How the history of blackface is rooted in racism" *History.com*, 15 Feb. 2019, https://www.history.com/news/blackface-history-racism-origins.

CNN Editorial Research. "Trayvon Martin shooting fast facts." *CNN.com,* 17 Feb. 2021, https://www.cnn.com/2013/06/05/us/trayvon-martin-shooting-fast-facts/index.html.

Cole, Rachel, ed. "Solomon Northup. Encyclopedia Britannica.", 6 July 2020, https://www.britannica.com/biography/Solomon-Northup.

Constitutional Rights Foundation. "BRIA 14 3 a How welfare began in the United States.", 2021, https://www.crf-usa.org/bill-of-rights-in-action/bria-14-3-a-how-welfare-began-in-the-united-states.html.

Corliss, Richard. "D. W. Griffith's The Birth of a Nation 100 years later: still great, still shameful." *Time Magazine,* 3 March 2015, https://time.com/3729807/d-w-griffiths-the-birth-of-a-nation-10/.

De Faakto. "Native American warfare culture, how it influenced small wars, modern guerrilla warfare and special operations.", 4 May 2020, http://defaakto.com/2020/05/24/native-american-warfare-culture-how-it-influenced-small-wars-modern-guerrilla-warfare-and-special-operations/.

Delaney, Ruth, ed. "American History, race, and prison." https://www.vera.org/reimagining-prison-web-report/american-history-race-and-prison.

"Detroit"., 2017, https://www.historyvshollywood.com/reelfaces/detroit/.

Devine, Shane. "Fact check: do whites make up the largest share of food stamps, medicaid recipients?", 18 Oct. 2018, https://checkyourfact.com/2018/10/18/fact-check-whites-medicaid-food-stamps/.

Digital History. "The middle passage.", 2019, http://www.digitalhistory.uh.edu/disp_textbook.cfm?smtid=2&psid=446.

Digital History. "What was lifelike under slavery.", 2019, http://www.digitalhistory.uh.edu/disp_textbook.cfm?smtID=2&psid=3040.

Dokosi, Michael Eli. "A look at the Casual Killing Act of 1669 that made it legal to kill a slave at will.", 23 Nov. 2019, *https://face2faceafrica.com/article/a-look-at-the-casual-killing-act-of-1669-that-made-it-legal-to-kill-a-slave-at-will.*

Domonoske, Camila. "Segregated from its history, how "ghetto" lost its meaning". NPR, 27 April 2014, https://www.npr.org/sections/codeswitch/2014/04/27/306829915/segregated-from-its-history-how-ghetto-lost-its-meaning.

Dresser, Madge. "Bristol and the Transatlantic slave trade." https://www.bristolmuseums.org.uk/stories/bristol-transatlantic-slave-trade/.

Drucker, Jesse, ed. How Trump tax break to help poor communities became a windfall for the rich. *The New York Times,* 31 Aug. 2019, https://www.nytimes.com/2019/08/31/business/tax-opportunity-zones.html.

ReMastered: the two killings of Sam Cooke. Directed by Kelly Duane de la Vega, Netflix, 2019.

Elfrink, Tim. "Open up the case, period": Sandra Bland's family demands answers over new video of her arrest". *The Washington* Post, 7 May 2019, https://www.washingtonpost.com/nation/2019/05/07/open-up-case-period-sandra-blands-family-demands-answers-over-new-video-her-arrest/.

Elliot, Jane. "Jane Elliot.", 2019, https://janeelliott.com/.

Ely, Danielle. M., Driscoll, Anne. "Infant mortality in the United States, 2017: Data from the period linked birth/infant death file." *National Vital Statistics Reports,* vol. 6, no. 10, 2019, https://www.cdc.gov/nchs/data/nvsr/nvsr68/nvsr68_10-508.pdf.

"Emmett Till murderers make magazine confession". History.com. https://www.history.com/this-day-in-history/emmett-till-murderers-make-magazine-confession.

Encyclopedia.com. "Assata Shakur.", 1 March 2020, https://www.encyclopedia.com/history/historians-and-chronicles/historians-miscellaneous-biographies/assata-shakur.

Enouen, Susan. "New research shows Planned Parenthood targets minority neighborhoods.", 1 Oct. 2012, https://www.lifeissues.org/2012/10/new-research-shows-planned-parenthood-targets-minority-neighborhoods/.

ESPN. "Colin Kaepernick protests anthem over treatment of minorities.", 27 August 2016, https://theundefeated.com/features/colin-kaepernick-protests-anthem-over-treatment-of-minorities/.

EyeWitness to History. "Aboard a slave ship, 1829.", 2000, http://www.eyewitnesstohistory.com/slaveship.htm.

Fain, Kimberly. "The devastation of Black Wall Street.", 5 July 2017, https://daily.jstor.org/the-devastation-of-black-wall-street/.

Friedersdorf, Conor. "The audacity of talking about race with the Ku Klux Klan." *The Atlantic*, 27 March 2015, https://www.theatlantic.com/politics/archive/2015/03/the-audacity-of-talking-about-race-with-the-klu-klux-klan/388733/.

Gates, Henry Louis. Jr. "100 amazing facts about the Negro." *PBS*. https://www.pbs.org/wnet/african-americans-many-rivers-to-cross/history/the-truth-behind-40-acres-and-a-mule/.

Ghansah, Rachel Kaadzi. "A most American terrorist: the making of Dylann Roof." *GQ* Magazine, 21 Aug. 2017, https://www.gq.com/story/dylann-roof-making-of-an-american-terrorist.

Glenza, Jessica. "Rosewood massacre a harrowing tale of racism and the road toward reparations." *The Guardian,* 3 Jan. 2016, https://www.theguardian.com/us-news/2016/jan/03/rosewood-florida-massacre-racial-violence-reparations.

"Gu" (Ogun): The God of Iron."

http://www.mamiwata.com/ogun.html.

Hauser, Christine. Florida woman whose "Stand Your Ground" defense was rejected is released. *The New York Times,* 7 Feb. 2017, https://www.nytimes.com/2017/02/07/us/marissa-alexander-released-stand-your-ground.html.

Henry, Carma. "Research reveals that Black children were fed to hogs and used as alligator bait in the early 1900s.", 6 July 2019, https://thewestsidegazette.com/research-reveals-that-black-children-were-fed-to-hogs-and-used-as-alligator-bait-in-the-early-1900s/.

"Hip hop is born at a birthday party in the Bronx". History.com. https://www.history.com/this-day-in-history/hip-hop-is-born-at-a-birthday-party-in-the-bronx.

Hiskey, Daven. "Did people in medieval times really not bathe?", 26 Aug. 2019, http://www.todayifoundout.com/index.php/2019/08/did-people-in-medieval-times-really-not-bathe/.

History Making Productions. "Samuel Hopkins granted first patent in the United States." *The Philadelphia Inquirer,* 31 July 2013, https://www.inquirer.com/philly/blogs/TODAY-IN-PHILADELPHIA-HISTORY/Samuel-Hopkins-granted-first-patent-in-the-United-States.html.

History.com (Ed.). "Abraham Lincoln's Assassination.", 27 Oct. 2009, https://www.history.com/topics/american-civil-war/abraham-lincoln-assassination.

History.com (Ed.). "Brown v. Board of Education.", 27 Oct. 2009, https://www.history.com/topics/black-history/brown-v-board-of-education-of-topeka.
History.com (Ed.). "Civil Rights Movement.", 27 Oct. 2009, https://www.history.com/topics/black-history/civil-rights-movement.
History.com (Ed.). "Ku Klux Klan.", 29 Oct. 2009, https://www.history.com/topics/reconstruction/ku-klux-klan.
History.com (Ed.). "NAACP", 29 Oct. 2009, https://www.history.com/topics/civil-rights-movement/naacp.
History.com (Ed.). "Underground Railroad.", 29 Oct. 2009, https://www.history.com/topics/black-history/underground-railroad.
History.com (Ed.). "Birmingham church bombing.", 27 Jan. 2010, https://www.history.com/topics/1960s/birmingham-church-bombing.
History.com (Ed.). "Sharecropping.", 24 June 2010, https://www.history.com/topics/black-history/sharecropping.
History.com (Ed.). "Cotton gin and Eli Whitney.", 10 Oct. 2010, https://www.history.com/topics/inventions/cotton-gin-and-eli-whitney.
History.com (Ed.). "Apartheid.", 7 Oct. 2010, https://www.history.com/topics/africa/apartheid.
History.com (Ed.). "War on drugs.", 31 May 2017, https://www.history.com/topics/crime/the-war-on-drugs.
History.com (Ed.). "Black Panthers.", 3 Nov. 0217, https://www.history.com/topics/civil-rights-movement/black-panthers.

History.com (Ed.). "Manifest Destiny.", 15 Nov. 2019, https://www.history.com/topics/westward-expansion/manifest-destiny.

History.com (Ed.). "Black codes.", 21 Jan. 2021, https://www.history.com/topics/black-history/black-codes.

History.com (Ed.). "Civil war." https://www.history.com/topics/american-civil-war/american-civil-war-history.

Hopkins, Samuel, Maxey, David. "Samuel Hopkins, the holder of the first U.S. patent: A study of failure." *The Pennsylvania Magazine of History and Biography,* vol.122, no. ½, 1998, pp. 3-37. http://www.jstor.org/stable/20093186.

How "Christianity is the white man's religion" feeds the damaging disconnect between the Diaspora and Africa.", 28 Feb. 2018, http://blackyouthproject.com/christianity-white-mans-religion-feeds-damaging-disconnect-diaspora-africa/.

Hughes, F. "The African dodger.", Oct. 2012, https://www.ferris.edu/HTMLS/news/jimcrow/question/2012/october.htm.

Jager, Chris. "Are the crows in Dumbo really that racist?", 19 Dec. 2019, https://www.lifehacker.com.au/2019/12/ask-lh-are-the-crows-in-dumbo-racist/.

Jarus, Owen. "Ancient Egypt: a brief history.", 28 July 2016, https://www.livescience.com/55578-egyptian-civilization.html.

Jeffries, Bayyinah S. "Oshun." Encyclopedia Britannica., 3 Sept. 2017, https://www.britannica.com/topic/Oshun.

Jencks, Christopher, Phillips, Meredith. "The Black-White test score gap: why it persists and what can be done.", 1 March 1998, https://www.brookings.edu/articles/the-black-white-test-score-gap-why-it-persists-and-what-can-be-done/.

Jenkins, John Philip. "White supremacy. Encyclopedia Britannica.", 30 Nov. 2016, https://www.britannica.com/topic/white-supremacy.

Johnson, Elizabeth Ofosuah. "The disturbing history of enslaved mothers forced to breastfeed white babies in the 1600s.", 20 Aug. 2018, https://face2faceafrica.com/article/the-disturbing-history-of-enslaved-mothers-forced-to-breastfeed-white-babies-in-the-1600s.

Johnson, Elizabeth Ofosuah. "5 horrifying ways enslaved African men were sexually exploited and abused by their white masters.", 11 Oct. 2018, https://face2faceafrica.com/article/5-horrifying-ways-enslaved-african-men-were-sexually-exploited-and-abused-by-their-white-masters/3.

Johnson, Shontavia. "America's always had black inventors – even when the patent system explicitly excluded them.", 14 Feb. 2017, https://theconversation.com/americas-always-had-black-inventors-even-when-the-patent-system-explicitly-excluded-them-72619.

Johnson, Theodore. III. "Recall that ice cream truck song? We have unpleasant news for you." *NPR*, 11 May 2014,https://www.npr.org/sections/codeswitch/2014/05/11/310708342/recall-that-ice-cream-truck-song-we-have-unpleasant-news-for-you,

Jones, Monique. "8 films that use a white savior as a major plot device.", 13 March 2019, https://shadowandact.com/films-white-savior-plot-devices.

Joseph, Seb. "Advertising, mired in racism, has a long road to recovery.", 5 June 2020, https://digiday.com/media/advertising-mired-in-racism-has-a-long-road-to-recovery/.

Kaelber, Lutz. "Eugenics/sexual sterilizations in North Carolina.", 30 Oct. 2014, https://www.uvm.edu/~lkaelber/eugenics/NC/NC.html.

Keener, Craig. "The Maafa or African Holocaust." http://nationaljuneteenth.com/Maafa.html.

Keneally, Meghan. "What to know about the violent Charlottesville protests and anniversary rallies." *ABC News*, 8 Aug. 2018, https://abcnews.go.com/US/happen-charlottesville-protest-anniversary-weekend/story?id=57107500.

Kettler, Sara. "7 facts on George Washington Carver." *Bioagraphy.com*, 1 March 2015, https://www.biography.com/news/george-washington-carver-facts-national-peanut-month.

Kifner, John. "FBI sought doom of Panther party." *The New York Times*, 9 May 1976, https://www.nytimes.com/1976/05/09/archives/fbi-sought-doom-of-panther-party-senate-study-says-plot-led-to.html..

Kiger, Patrick. "Did colonist give infected blankets to Native Americans as biological warfare?", *25 Nov. 2019,* https://www.history.com/news/colonists-native-americans-smallpox-blankets

Klein, Christopher. "How Selma's "Bloody Sunday" became a turning point in the Civil Rights Movement." *History.com*, 6 March 2015, https://www.history.com/news/selma-bloody-sunday-attack-civil-rights-movement.

Bullock Allen, ed. "Adolf Hitler." *Encyclopedia Britannica*, 26 April 2020, https://www.britannica.com/biography/Adolf-Hitler.

Koerner, Brendan. "Why does the Ku Klux Klan burn crosses?" *Slate News*, 17 Dec. 2002, https://slate.com/news-and-politics/2002/12/why-does-the-ku-klux-klan-burn-crosses.html.

Ktitowsky. "Phrenology and "scientific racism" in the 19th century." *Real Archaeology*, 5 March 2017, https://pages.vassar.edu/realarchaeology/2017/03/05/phrenology-and-scientific-racism-in-the-19th-century/.

Lack, Caleb. "Mammy, Jezebel, Sapphire, or Queen? Stereotypes of the African-American female.", 28 April 2015, https://skepticink.com/gps/2015/04/28/mammy-jezebel-sapphire-or-queen-stereotypes-of-the-african-american-female/.

Landry. "Paying to play Indian: the Dawes rolls and the legacy of $5 Indians.", 21 March 2017, https://indiancountrytoday.com/archive/paying-to-play-indian-the-dawes-rolls-and-the-legacy-of-5-indians-3yha0LldYUaH7smRsrks8A.

Latson, Jennifer. "What Margaret Sanger really said about eugenics and race." *Time*, 14 Oct. 2016, https://time.com/4081760/margaret-sanger-history-eugenics/.

Lawrence, Tyler Marie. "5 nursery songs that are actually really racist and should be removed from every child's learning routine." *Blavity News*, 4 Oct. 2019, https://blavity.com/blavity-original/5-nursery-songs-that-are-actually-really-racist-and-should-be-removed-from-every-childs-learning-routine?category1=culture.

Legal Information Institute. "Affirmative Action." https://www.law.cornell.edu/wex/affirmative_action.

Lexington Law. "Important welfare statistics for 2021", 5 Feb. 2021, https://www.lexingtonlaw.com/blog/finance/welfare-statistics.html.

Library of Congress. "Voting rights for African Americans." https://www.loc.gov/classroom-materials/elections/right-to-vote/voting-rights-for-african-americans/%23:~:text=In%201965%2C%20the%20Voting%20Rights,African%20Americans%20throughout%20the%20South.

Light, A. "Hip-hop." https://www.britannica.com/art/hip-hop.

Lopez, German. "Philando Castile Minnesota police shooting: officer cleared of manslaughter charge." *Vox*, 16 June 2017, https://www.vox.com/2016/7/7/12116288/minnesota-police-shooting-philando-castile-falcon-heights-video.

Lopez, German. "Cleveland just fired the cop who shot and killed 12-year-old Tamir Rice more than 2 years ago." *Vox*, 30 May 2017, https://www.vox.com/identities/2017/5/30/15713254/cleveland-police-tamir-rice-timothy-loehmann.

Lussana, Sergio. "To See Who Was Best on the Plantation: Enslaved Fighting Contests and Masculinity in the Antebellum Plantation South." *The Journal of Southern History*, vol. 76, no. 4, 2010, pp. 901-922. from http://www.jstor.org/stable/27919283.

MacGuill, Dan. "Was a violently racist carnival game once popular in America?", 26 Feb. 2018, https://www.snopes.com/fact-check/racist-carnival-game/.

"Malcom X Quotable Quotes." https://www.goodreads.com/quotes/89182-if-someone-puts-their-hands-on-you-make-sure-they.

Margaret Sanger to Dr. C. J. Gamble, 1930 December 30, *A Negro project letter*, https://libex.smith.edu/omeka/files/original/d6358bc3053c93183295bf2df1c0c931.pdf.

Mark, Joshua. "Ancient Egypt.", 2 Sept. 2009, https://www.ancient.eu/egypt/.

Mark, Joshua. "Egyptian book of the dead.", 24 March 2016, *https://www.ancient.eu/Egyptian_Book_of_the_Dead/.*

Mark, Joshua. "Alexander the Great.", 14 Nov. 2013, https://www.ancient.eu/Alexander_the_Great/.

Martschenko, Daphne. The IQ test wars: why screening for intelligence is still so controversial.", 10 Oct. 2017, https://theconversation.com/the-iq-test-wars-why-screening-for-intelligence-is-still-so-controversial-81428.

Matchar, Emily. "The first African-American to hold a patent invented "Dry Scouring". *Smithsonian* Magazine, 27 Feb. 2019, https://www.smithsonianmag.com/innovation/first-african-american-hold-patent-invented-dry-scouring-180971394/.

Melton, J. Gordon. "Nation of Islam." *Encyclopedia Britannica,* 1 Oct. 2020, https://www.britannica.com/topic/Nation-of-Islam.

Mendelson, Scott. "Lionsgate responds to "Gods of Egypt". *Forbes,* 27 Nov. 2015, https://www.forbes.com/sites/scottmendelson/2015/11/27/exclusive-lionsgate-responds-to-gods-of-egypt-whitewashing-controversy/?sh=164be97fcd02.

Merelli, Annalisa. "The darker your skin the more likely you'll end up in an American jail.", 16 Oct. 2019, https://qz.com/1724590/colorism-influences-probability-of-going-to-jail-new-study-finds/.

Miletich, Steve. "Family, Seattle police prepare for inquest into fatal shooting of Charleena Lyles." *Seattle Times,* 10 Sept. 2019, https://www.seattletimes.com/seattle-news/crime/family-seattle-police-prepare-for-inquest-into-fatal-shooting-of-charleena-lyles/.

Miller, Brad. "Fast food versus grocery store.", 16 July 2012, https://ucanr.edu/blogs/blogcore/postdetail.cfm?postnum=7935.

Miller, Tamiyah. "Skin lightening, bleaching, whiting phenomenon" (Publication No. 732), 2011, [Master's thesis, Gettysburg College]. https://cupola.gettysburg.edu/student_scholarship/732.

Mohamud, Naima. "Is Mansa Munsa the richest man who ever lived?", 10 March 2019, https://www.bbc.com/news/world-africa-47379458.

Mokoena, Hlonipha. "From slavery to colonialism and school rules, navigating the history of myths about black hair.", 24 Feb. 2018, https://qz.com/africa/1215070/black-hair-myths-from-slavery-to-colonialism-school-rules-and-good-hair/.

Monk, Ellis. "The color of punishment: African Americans, skin tone, and the criminal justice system." *Ethnic and Racial Studies,* vol. 42, no.10, 2018, pp. 1593-1612. https://doi.org/10.1080/01419870.2018.1508736.

Müller-Wille, Staffan. "Carolus Linnaeus." *Encyclopedia Britannica,* 7 Jan. 2021. https://www.britannica.com/biography/Carolus-Linnaeus.

NAACP. "The significance of "The Doll Test". https://www.naacpldf.org/ldf-celebrates-60th-anniversary-brown-v-board-education/significance-doll-test/.

National Archives. "Fred Hampton." https://www.archives.gov/research/african-americans/individuals/fred-hampton.

National Park Service. "Seneca Village, New York City." https://www.nps.gov/articles/seneca-village-new-york-city.htm.

Nobel Lecture. "Martin Luther King Jr.", 18 Feb. 2021, https://www.nobelprize.org/prizes/peace/1964/king/lecture/.

NYCLU. "Stop and frisk data." https://www.nyclu.org/en/stop-and-frisk-data.

Odutayo, D. "Rwanda deploys officials to enforce ban on skin lightening creams." *CNN*.com, 9 Jan. 2019, https://www.cnn.com/2019/01/09/health/rwanda-ban-skin-lightening-cream-africa-intl/index.html.

"Jane Elliott's "Blue Eyes/Brown Eyes" anti-racism exercise | the Oprah Winfrey show". *Youtube*, uploaded by OWN, 5 June 2020, https://www.youtube.com/watch?app=desktop&v=ebPoSMULI5U&feature=youtu.be.

Panetta, Grace, Collman, Ashley. "The life and career of Candace Owens, the Black conservative activist who attached Black Lives Matter and said George Floyd was "not a good person". *Business Insider*, 13 June 2020, https://www.businessinsider.com/candace-owens-black-conservative-activist-life-career-attacks-2020-6.

Perez-Pena, Richard. "Woman linked to 1955 Emmett Till murder tells historian her claims were false." *The New York* Times, 27 Jan. 2017, https://www.nytimes.com/2017/01/27/us/emmett-till-lynching-carolyn-bryant-donham.html.

Pflum, Mary. "Mom jailed for lying to get kids in better school speaks out on college scandal." *Today.*, 15 March 2019, https://www.today.com/parents/ohio-mom-jailed-school-swap-college-cheating-scandal-t150441.

Pilgrim, David. "The coon caricature.", Oct. 2000, https://www.ferris.edu/jimcrow/coon/.

Pilgrim, David. "Nigger and caricature.", Sept. 2001, https://www.ferris.edu/HTMLS/news/jimcrow/caricature/homepage.htm.

Posner, Liz. "The green rush is too white." *Pacific Standard* Magazine, 10 Dec. 2018, https://psmag.com/economics/the-green-rush-is-too-white-hood-incubator-race-weed.

Pruitt, Sarah. "5 things you may not know about Abraham Lincoln, slavery and emancipation." *History.com*, 21 Sept. 2015, https://www.history.com/news/5-things-you-may-not-know-about-lincoln-slavery-and-emancipation.

Quasibah. "Manifesting reality." https://ancestralvoices.co.uk/manifesting-reality/.

Randall, Vernellia. "Mammy Jezebel and Sistahs", 1 April 2012, https://racism.org/index.php?option=com_content&view=article&id=1277:aawomen01a&catid=72&Itemid=215.

Reece, Robert. "Genesis of U.S. colorism and skin tone stratification: Slavery freedom, and Mulatto-Black occupational inequity in the late 19th century." *The Review of Black Political Economy,* vol. 45, no. 1, 2018, pp. 3-21. https://doi.org/10.1177/0034644618770761.

Reid, Jason. "Eric Reid, Coling Kaepernick united in legal battle against NFL.", 3 May 2018, https://theundefeated.com/features/eric-reid-colin-kaepernick-united-in-legal-battle-against-nfl/.

Roberts, Leon. "How Black Lives Matter changed the way Americans fight for freedom.", 13 July 2018, https://www.aclu.org/blog/racial-justice/race-and-criminal-justice/how-black-lives-matter-changed-way-americans-fight.

Robinson, Trevor. "A brief rundown of racism within advertising and why it's still happening today.", 21 Feb. 2019, https://www.adweek.com/agencies/a-brief-rundown-of-racism-within-advertising-and-why-its-still-happening-today/.

Roeder, Amy. "America is failing its black mothers." *Harvard Public Health* Magazine, 2019, https://www.hsph.harvard.edu/magazine/magazine_article/america-is-failing-its-black-mothers/.

"Sara "Saartjie" Baartman." *The South African History Online.* https://www.sahistory.org.za/people/sara-saartjie-baartman.

Sastry, Anjuli, Bates, Karen. "When LA erupted in anger: a look back at the Rodney King riots" *NPR*, 26 April 2017, https://www.npr.org/2017/04/26/524744989/when-la-erupted-in-anger-a-look-back-at-the-rodney-king-riots.

Savage, John. ""Black Magic" and White Terror: Slave Poisoning and Colonial Society in Early 19th Century Martinique." *Journal of Social History,* vol.40, no. (3), 2007, pp. 635-662. http://www.jstor.org/stable/4491942.

Savali, Kirsten West. "Did you know? US Gov't found guilty in conspiracy to assassinate Dr. Martin Luther King Jr." *Newsone*.com, 18 Jan. 2021, https://newsone.com/2843790/did-you-know-us-govt-found-guilty-in-conspiracy-to-assassinate-dr-martin-luther-king-jr/.

Scranton, Laird. "Shango." *Encyclopedia* Britannica, 1 Nov. 2016, https://www.britannica.com/topic/Shango.

Sentinel, Orlando. "Florida teen Trayvon Martin is shot and killed." *History.com*, 26 Feb. 2012, https://www.history.com/this-day-in-history/florida-teen-trayvon-martin-is-shot-and-killed.

Shelton, Malik. "The emasculation of the Black Man in the entertainment industry.", *2013,* http://www.timbooktu.com/shelton/emascblk.htm.

"Slavery before the Trans-Atlantic trade." http://ldhi.library.cofc.edu/exhibits/show/africanpassageslowcountryadapt/introductionatlanticworld/slaverybeforetrade.

Smith, Stephen, Ellis, Kate. "Shackled legacy. History shows slavery helped build many U.S. colleges and universities.", 4 Sept. 2017, *https://www.apmreports.org/episode/2017/09/04/shackled-legacy.*

Smithsonian. "Blackface: the birth of an American stereotype." National Museum of African American History & Culture. https://nmaahc.si.edu/blog-post/blackface-birth-american-stereotype.

Snider, Amber. "The history of Yemaya, Santeria's queenly ocean goddess mermaid.", 9 July 2019, https://www.teenvogue.com/story/the-history-of-yemaya-goddess-mermaid.

Somerville, Diane. "Rape, race, and castration in slave law in the colonial and early South." *Oxford Scholarship*, 2011, DOI:10.1093/acprof:oso/9780195112436.003.0006.

Spivey, William. "The truth about American slave breeding farms.", 9 June 2019, https://medium.com/the-aambc-journal/the-truth-about-american-slave-breeding-farms-ee631e863e2c.

Statista Research Department. "Child abuse rate in the United States in 2019, by race/ethnicity of the victim.", Jan. 2021, https://www.statista.com/statistics/254857/child-abuse-rate-in-the-us-by-race-ethnicity/.

Sterling, Erica. "Maceo Snipes." https://coldcases.emory.edu/maceo-snipes/.

Stockton, Richard. "Why isn't Belgium's King Leopold II as reviled as Hitler or Stalin?", 16 Sept. 2016, https://allthatsinteresting.com/king-leopold-ii-congo.

Takei, Carl. "President Trump, stop and frisk is both unconstitutional and ineffective.", 9 Oct. 2018, https://www.aclu.org/blog/criminal-law-reform/reforming-police/president-trump-stop-and-frisk-both-unconstitutional-and.

"The abolition of the slave trade." *The New York Public Library*, 2012, https://wayback.archive-

it.org/13235/20200727201752/http://abolition.nypl.org/home/.
"The African diaspora", http://www.experience-africa.de/index.php?en_the-african-diaspora.
"The Birst of a Nation opens, glorifying the KKK." History.com. https://www.history.com/this-day-in-history/birth-of-a-nation-opens.
"The Dawes Act." https://www.khanacademy.org/humanities/us-history/the-gilded-age/american-west/a/the-dawes-act.
"The Seminole wars." , 2021, https://dos.myflorida.com/florida-facts/florida-history/seminole-history/the-seminole-wars/.
The White House Historical Association. "Did slaves build the White House?" https://www.whitehousehistory.org/did-slaves-build-the-white-house.
The White House, Office of the Press Secretary. "President Donald J. Trump is lifting up American communities that have been left behind" [Press briefing], 12 Dec. 2018, https://www.ncsha.org/wp-content/uploads/2018-12-12-President-Donald-J.-Trump-Is-Lifting-Up-American-Communities-that-Have-Been-Left-Behind-%E2%80%93-The-White-House.pdf.
"This day in history: Columbus discovers America 1492." , 12 Oct. 2016, https://historycollection.co/day-history-columbus-discovers-america-1492/.
Three Initiates. (1912). "The Kybalion.".
"Tim Wise." https://www.speakoutnow.org/speaker/wise-tim.
"Timeline of events in shooting of Michael Brown in Ferguson." *AP News*, 8 Aug. 2019,

https://apnews.com/article/9aa32033692547699a3b61da8fd1fc62..
Tinubu, Aramide. "Disney's racist cartoons won't just stay hidden in the vault. But they could be used as a teachable moment." *NBC News*, 15 April 2019, https://www.nbcnews.com/think/opinion/disney-s-racist-cartoons-won-t-just-stay-hidden-vault-ncna998216.
U.S. History. "54h. Malcom X and the Nation of Islam." https://www.ushistory.org/us/54h.asp.
United States Census Bureau. "United States quick facts." https://www.census.gov/quickfacts/fact/table/US/IPE120219.
United States Department of Health and Human Services Office of Minority Health. "Infant mortality and African Americans." https://minorityhealth.hhs.gov/omh/browse.aspx?lvl=4&lvlid=23.
Urofsky, Melvin. "Jim Crow law". *Encyclopedia Britannica,* 12 Feb. 2021, https://www.britannica.com/event/Jim-Crow-law.
Vice Staff. "Coloring the Black Panthers." *Vice News*, 26 Oct. 2010, https://www.vice.com/en/article/3bpxek/coloring-the-black-panthers.

Villarosa, Linda. "Myths about physical racial differences were used to justify slavery – and are still believed by doctors today." *The New York Times Magazine*, 14 Aug. 2019, https://www.nytimes.com/interactive/2019/08/14/magazine/racial-differences-doctors.html.

Voncujovi, Sena. "How African spirituality got tied to Satan.", 30 June 2020, https://humanparts.medium.com/why-african-spirituality-became-associated-with-satan-a16712cf9cdf.

Wade, Michael. "Johnny Rebel and the Cajun Roots of right-wing rock." *Popular Music and Society,* vol. 30, no. 4, 2008, https://doi.org/10.1080/03007760701546364.

Waxman, Olivia. "The first Africans in Virginia landed in 1619. It was a turning point for slavery in American history - but not the beginning.", 20 Aug. 2019, https://time.com/5653369/august-1619-jamestown-history/.

Wilkinson, Kate. "Fact sheet: South Africa's official poverty numbers.", 15 Feb. 2018, https://africacheck.org/fact-checks/factsheets/factsheet-south-africas-official-poverty-numbers.

Williams, Monnica. "How White feminists oppress Black women: When feminism functions as white supremacy.", 16 Jan. 2019, https://chacruna.net/how-white-feminists-oppress-black-women-when-feminism-functions-as-white-supremacy/.

Wilson, Sacoby, Carter, Sakereh, "Let's talk about scientific racism, colonialism, and imperialism.", 14 Sept. 2020, https://ceejhlab.medium.com/lets-talk-about-scientific-racism-colonialism-and-imperialism-952c3bb938cf.

Wolfe, Brendan. "Thrown to the sharks.", 9 Jan. 2012, https://evblog.virginiahumanities.org/2012/01/thrown-to-the-sharks/.

"World War II." *History.com.* https://www.history.com/topics/world-war-ii.

Index

About the Author

A Washington D.C. and S.C. native, **Rodney Cloud Hill** served six years in the United States Air Force. His military career allowed him the opportunity to experience the world. While serving, he finished his bachelor's degree in Sociology, where he gained a passion for knowledge and aspirations to heal the Black community. Hill is a member of two Fraternal organizations that does such, Kappa Alpha Psi Fraternity, Inc. and Prince Hall Free and Accepted Masonry.

Today, Rodney Cloud Hill is most recognized for his first published book, "The Cloud Effect", available on Amazon, as well as his event coordination and performances of "Third Eye Sessions".

Third Eye Sessions is an exposition founded by Mr. Hill where inspiration, education, and entertainment intertwine through various forms of art. Third Eye Sessions spread consciousness and a sense of connection with The Universe, while promoting the talents and creativity of the community. Its mission is to make sure you leave each event venue with a broader spectrum of reality as well as being entertained.

Hill is intensely passionate about the education and livelihood of his fellow men and women. He has spoken at college campuses and participated on panels discussing an array of societal issues. He frequently works in the community supporting social activism, fighting to make a positive impact on society.

Made in the USA
Middletown, DE
27 August 2021